IVY'S TURN

IVY'S TURN

David Updike

PENNINGTON PRESS

To order additional copies of this book, contact:
Xlibris Corporation
1-888-795-4274
www.Xlibris.com
Orders@Xlibris.com
29909

Contents

For Wesley,
a wonderful son,
at sixteen.

With thanks to the readers
who offered suggestions and corrections:
Jin Auh, Emily Donaldson, Wambui Githiora-Updike,
Marsha Meade, Sendy Jean.
And special thanks to Miranda Updike
for painting Ivy, swiftly and beautifully;
and to my many wonderful students at
Roxbury Community College,
who offer inspiration and encouragement
without even knowing it.

Readers interested in communicating with the author may do so by e-mail:
DVDUPD@aol.com

Fall

It was the kind of morning that could make you slightly nervous—clear and sunny and cool, the grass wet with dew, a few leaves on the trees touched with the red and yellow of the coming fall. Here and there clumps of teenagers drifted along the sidewalks in their new clothes, talking and laughing as they walked. It was already early October, but everything still had a feeling of newness, strangeness, and every day as he walked to school it seemed like it was for the first time.

The sidewalks of the city were brick, mostly, the color of rust, worn smooth from years of stepping, shuffling feet. In places the roots of trees had pushed the bricks up into little hills and valleys, and if you weren't careful you could trip and stumble on a brick raised slightly higher than the others. As Zak crossed the park that led into the school this morning, he could hear the disparate strains of Spanish, Creole, and English.

"Yo, Zak," someone said to him now, as he crossed a little park and came up to the school. "What's up?" It was Herman, a tall, thin Black kid who had taken an amused interest in him for some reason, and as he passed he held out a hand to shake, or rather, a fist to bump. "What's up, Herman?"

"Not much, Hayseed. Just chillin'." Although Zak didn't much care for the nickname, he didn't mind it from Herman, maybe because he knew that Herman liked him, and being liked by Herman saved him some trouble with some of Herman's friends who didn't seem to share his affection.

Inside, the hallways of the high school were quiet, more or less—a few kids drifting along, a teacher or two, a locker door slamming shut, the laughter of teenaged girls. Zak hung up his coat, got his books and went on into homeroom where a handful of kids were littered around the room, looking sleepy.

"Good morning, Zachary," Mr. Turnbull said.

"Good morning." He sat down at his usual cluster of desks, across from Tom Dunn, a chubby kid with glasses whose father owned a gas station over in East Carver. "Hey, Zakster," he said. "Hey, Tom. How are you doing?"

"Good. Flunking out."

"Great. Your parents must be happy."

"My dad doesn't care. He just wants me to come work in the gas station and forget about school, wrestle with bolts and be a grease monkey for the rest of my life."

"Good idea," said Zak. "Maybe I'll join you." The clock in the room was one of those that jumped, suddenly, from one minute to the next, and Zak happened to look up just at the instant it leapt from 8:13 to 8:14, followed by the sound of music, some vaguely familiar song drifting out of the intercom. Years before, back in the seventies, some hippy principal had replaced the clanging of the bell with music, so the end and beginning of classes were now announced by a fifteen-second segment of a song.

The room was filling up—noisy kids, quiet kids, laughing kids, a trio of pretty girls, dull-looking pimply boys, two girls talking Spanish, their stomachs showing—everyone in the eleventh grade whose names began with the letters T through Z. At 8:22, exactly, Mr. Turnbull took out his book and started reading down the list of names, and as he got closer to Walker, Zak could feel himself getting slightly nervous, as if, when the time came he would forget how to answer.

"Vipond, David."

"Eek—I mean, here."

"Walker, Zachary." he finally said. Zak was ready.

"Here." Now, he could relax.

"Waller, Nancy."

"Yes."

"Whitman, Ivy," he said, but there was no answer.

"No Ivy today? That's lamentable—so much for perfect attendance." He was about to put a red mark in his book when someone came rushing in, said "Here," and walked quickly toward an empty seat.

"Tardy!" Mr. Turnbull said happily, looking down and frowning while this girl named Ivy looked around, waved to her friends, and then sat down in the only available chair in the room, which happened to be across from Zak. She was panting slightly, and she muttered softly, to no one in particular, catching her breath. "I can't believe I made it. I missed the bus."

"Just in time," Zak said, surprised, as he usually didn't say much to girls. He had never really noticed her before, as she usually sat on the other side of the room.

"I ran," the girl said, taking off her coat, wiping the beads of sweat that had formed like pearls on her face. She had a high, smooth forehead, light brown eyes, her skin a slightly darker shade of brown. Her hair was held back from her face by a plastic hair band, blue, and her eyebrows formed soft and perfect arcs above her almond shaped eyes.

"Did I miss anything?" she asked, looking back at Zak, but it was a second before he realized she was talking to him.

"Not really," he said, and wanted to say something more, but what? In places her hair rose up above her head like shreds of clouds torn loose by the wind. Zak looked up in time to see the minute hand of the clock leap from 8:24 to 8:25, and a second later the music came on, a few lines of Public Enemy, without the "offensive language", and everyone moved to the door and swept, in one great, roiling mass of teenaged humanity, through the halls of the school.

Lies

Zak had never been too good around girls. He had always been shy and quiet, and never could think of what to say. Back in Vermont he had a girlfriend, of sorts, two years younger, and for a couple of months the previous summer they had driven around in the back of his friend's mother's car, drinking beer and making out and going to ninety-nine cent double features. Then he had gotten his own license, and for a couple of weeks before he was smuggled off to the city, he had driven around with her himself and parked at the few familiar places in town: at the back of an enormous cornfield, by the edge of Hosner's pond, in the dim lit parking lot behind the bowling alley. There, they would sit and listen to the radio, and kiss, and he would stroke the smooth, tanned skin of her stomach, and elsewhere, but not much more. His friends, he knew, had boasted of having "done it" up in the hayloft of their parents' barn, or in one of the cheap motels out on route nine, out towards Olney, but Zak had no particular desire to go out to one of these cheap motels, or to lose his virginity in the back of someone's crappy car. Besides, he wasn't quite sure he wanted to.

"It's like," one of his precocious friends had told him the previous summer, looking for the right words, "it's like this giant muscle has gotten hold of you, and won't let go!"—a prospect Zak did not find overly appealing.

From his first month Carver Central High School—some called it Carver, others Central—it was clear that Zaks' fellow students did not share his timidity. In the cafeteria, he had heard boys talking about who had "hooped" who over the weekend, and what had happened after so and so's party, and how some girl was having a baby "for Damian." He couldn't quite understand how you could have a baby "for" someone, as if it was a gift to be wrapped up like a Christmas present and handed over during recess. In any event, there was plenty of evidence of procreation at his new school—a day care center, for one thing, with lots of crying, snuffling, sleeping, squalling babies in it. After school the young mothers could be seen strolling around through the falling leaves, stopping to show off their bawling trophies to their friends. Sometimes boys hovered around in their long baggy pants and untied sneakers, quietly taking credit for this new person they had helped bring into the world. But when the young mothers finally headed off toward home, pushing the strollers before them, they usually did so alone, and the fathers hung back in the park, talking and laughing with their friends.

Zak wasn't doing particularly well in school that fall. The placement office had put him in a confusing jumble of classes—Math, English, Social Studies, French, and then some weird course for fuck-ups called "Contemporary Issues"; the teacher was a short, friendly man called Mr. Nicolosi, but any attempt to actually discuss contemporary issues was thwarted by a small bunch of assholes who sat in the back with their feet up, making life difficult. And he generally put up with their rudeness but now and then he would get angry and red faced and give someone detention, which made them all laugh. The leaders of this downwardly mobile crowd, as Zak had come to think of them, were two boys: Hector, a thin, tight lipped kid who liked to swear, and Anthony—a large boned, long haired Italian heavy metal freak who called the teacher Mr. Ralph. "Hey, Mr. Ralph," he would say. "You had a good weekend? You get *any*?" which Mr. Nicolosi, after ten or twenty years of this kind of thing, wanted to answer, "Yeah, with your mother." but smiled slightly instead.

Zak always sat near the front, though they had tried to draw him back into their part of the room. "Hey, Hayseed," they would say, "Come back with the bad boys. Don't you know this is the dumb class? You must have fucked up on the test."

"I guess so." Zak would say, and tried to ignore them. There were also a couple of noisy, cackling blond girls who used to pretend to touch Mr. Nicolosi's ass when he walked by them up the aisle. In the front of the room sat a few other kids who always did their homework and tried to keep the discussion going, and did all their assignments. Then there were the others—"the silent majority," as Mr. Nicolosi called them—who sat in the middle and watched, waiting to see who would win the struggle. But in truth Zak liked his new school, liked the great tumult of students—the boys in their big, baggy clothes, the girls with their earrings and nose rings and belly button rings, glinting from their smooth bellies; he liked the Asian students in their tight little clumps, and the Haitians and Latinos, the preppies and the freaks and the hangers-on, nerdy white kids who hung out in the computer lab and did their homework and worried about where they would get into college. He didn't care, much, for the bathroom crowd, kids who hung out there smoking cigarettes, and muttering little things to him about the way he was dressed, but he pretended not to hear them—just peed, glanced in the mirror to make sure his hair wasn't sticking up, and got out. When he had first arrived, he noticed that every time he walked past some Black kids he would get kind of nervous, like they were going to say something to him, or make fun of him, or jump him, or something, but after a week or two realized this was a lot of bull he had picked up from somewhere, and when he walked by nobody even noticed him. When school was over he spilled out with everyone else into the warm, autumn air, and headed toward home.

That's when he felt weird, and dreaded this walk back to the empty, rented half a house where only he and his mother lived. He didn't understand why his father had stayed behind in Vermont, and what was so important about his mother returning to school that she couldn't wait a couple of years until Zak had finished high school? His father, of course, had to stay behind for his job, but why had Zak not been invited to stay with him, and finish high school there with his old friends?

And so when he came to the end of the park, one day, he didn't turn left, toward home, but like a lemming followed the stream of students flowing in the direction of the subway.

"Hey, Hayseed," someone said behind him, and Zak turned to see the scruffy form of Nick Johnson jogging up behind him. Nick was one of those kids whose hormones were ahead of schedule, and while Zak couldn't grow enough whiskers to see in the mirror, Nick already had a full man's beard, and had grown it out in a kind of wispy blond goatee. He wore black jeans, and a leather coat, and a brown felt hat in the style of old gangster movies, and looked about four or five years older than he really was. He was panting from smoking too much.

"Where you heading, Zakster?" he said.

"Just walking."

"Cool. I hear you. Want a smoke?" he offered, and then when Zak shook him off, said "cool" again, nodding, and expertly tamped down the pack and sparked one up.

"What about you?" Zak asked.

"Over to the Pit. I need to chill for a while before I head home."

The Pit, Zak knew, was a little brick space by the subway station that had become a hangout for teenagers—boys with skateboards and girls with dyed red hair and earrings in their eyebrows and tongues, who wore giant black boots and plaid, Catholic school girl type skirts. They smoked a lot, too, cigarettes and weed, Zak guessed, and yelled and shouted and played loud music, and hugged each other, suddenly and passionately, for no apparent reason.

Nick walked with long, purposeful strides, as if in a great hurry to get somewhere, and blew out great purple plumes of smoke that rose over his head like the smokestack of a train. He was in Zak's history class, and more than once Zak had helped him with his homework—or, rather, 'lent' him his homework in the study period before class.

"How you doing in history?" Zak asked, and Nick laughed, and then coughed out a cloud of smoke.

"Don't ask," he said. "I think I flunked that last test. Anyway, who cares—it's all bullshit, anyway—lies."

"What do you mean?"

"History—that's not what really happened."

"No? What really happened, then?"

"Other stuff—bad shit. They just don't want us to know, or we'll join the movement."

Zak tried not to laugh. "What movement?"

"Yo, man. Don't they teach you anything up in there in the sticks? There's a revolution starting up—they just don't want anyone to know about it."

"Oh, yeah," Zak said, "A revolution of skateboarders?"

"Skateboarders carrying machetes, you mean." Nick added, and threw his cigarette with a disdainful, expert flick of his middle finger.

When they got to the Pit, they sat down on one of the granite steps in the sun, watching three long-haired freaks playing hacky sack; nearby, some older guy with a beard was playing guitar, and three girls with multiple piercings and tattered clothes were sitting on the ground with their legs crossed, smoking and looking at each other with strange, vacant eyes and creepy smiles.

"Why do girls always travel in threes?" Zak said. "You ever notice that?"

"Couldn't tell you, man. Self-defense, maybe."

"Against the revolution?"

"Yeah, the revolution, and horny men." Nick said. "Rapists and murderers and shit."

But it was oddly pleasant, there, Zak had to admit—the soft, October sunlight flooding down over the roofs, the sound of a guitar, people milling around, hanging out—better than going home to an empty house, anyway. Even a dog, wearing a red bandana for a collar, seemed happy, and kept barking with a kind of retarded half smile on its face. Nick was about to light up another cigarette when Zak said, for no particular reason, "Let me try one of those."

"Whoa, Zakster. Go for it—we have the rest of our life to quit."

The taste sucked, but Zak, not wanting to wimp out in front of Nick, kept at it, taking the smoke into his mouth, but trying not to let it get down his throat and make him gag.

Just then three girls walked past them, and he could tell by the way they walked, the languorous way their hips slid back and forth like metronomes, that they were hot—"fly," as they said here in the city. They carried their coats on their arms, loops of gold swung from their ears and glinted in the late autumn sun, their sweaters that clung to their bodies, and in their wake left an invisible swirling trail of fragrances—perfume, wool, shampoo. As they were about to turn and go down into the subway, one of them turned and glanced back at Zak, and in that instant he recognized her, but from where? But then he remembered the eyes, the hair with its strange, kinetic energy, lifted up like shreds of clouds, the pretty face of the girl from his homeroom—Ivy. He raised his hand in a feeble wave, but she didn't seem to see him. Nick hadn't noticed them at all, or pretended he didn't. "Come on, man," he said. "Let's go. This is no day for the Pit. Bad karma."

"Oh, yeah—bad vibe, dude—totally!" Zak said, and together they walked across the street, in the general direction of the river that flowed through the city on its way out to the sea.

Home

Ivy Whitman lived a couple of subway stops away from the school, on a street of triple-deckers overhung with maple trees. From the subway, she said goodbye to her friends and walked slowly through the yellow shadows, scuffling through the leaves like in some corny movie, a knapsack full of books tugging on her shoulders. She had tests that week, and had to study, needed to get good grades that year, but she had a pale, blue telephone in her room, a gift for her sixteenth birthday, and it rang a lot, and once she got started talking it was hard for her friends to stop, and some of them were not as worried about grades as she was. Yvonne wasn't worried at all; she was worried about boys, about who liked her most that week, who she thought was cute, and what so and so said to so and so during math class and what to wear to the parties she seemed to always be going to. She worked on weekends at her aunt's beauty salon, and most of the money she made there went to clothes—sneakers, jeans, black dresses that fit her luscious body like a glove. Her smooth skin, a few shades darker than Ivy's, glowed, and when she and Ivy walked home after school, it was to Yvonne that most of the attention was directed.

"Hey, beautiful, what's up? Where you going?"

"Away." She would answer. Cars honked, and slowed down; hopeful men leaned out the window and tried to talk to her. "Hey, sugar. Can I have some? Take my number."

"How can you stand it?" Ivy had asked her one day, and Yvonne had said, "It's alright with me, as long as they keep their hands off my butt. They just wish, that's all."

In the beauty shop the grown men, waiting for their wives and girlfriends, also said things, and into her hand slipped little pieces of paper with their phone numbers on them and the hopeful entreaty, "Call me." When they turned their backs she threw them into the trash—all except one, given to her by a tall, fine man in his early thirties with a soft, gentle voice and a beautiful smile, which she folded into her purse, and then forgot about; she found it a month later and threw it out.

But Ivy had admirers too, and some of the people she talked to at night were boys, but she had put off their invitations to dates, to the movies, or to meet them on the weekend, or to come over to their houses after school before their mothers and fathers got home from work. Her mother and aunts and grandmother and father had all told her to beware of men, sweet smiling boys bearing gifts, for they might give you something you don't really want. Ivy had no intention of going through college pushing a stroller, and her mother had told her she had no intention of raising any more children. "I've done my share," she was fond of saying. "If you make any mistakes, you're on your own." But Ivy was not likely to make any mistakes, of that kind at least; she had barely kissed a boy before, and on Monday mornings when her friends came in with stories about the weekend, who was with whom, and did what, Ivy just sat and listened.

She lived on the third floor of a green house with white trim, in a neat room painted the color blue of a robin's egg. There were pillows on the bed, and a couple of stuffed animals, and a poster of Michael Jackson on the wall, when he was still a kid, looking beautiful. On her desk was a small black and white photograph of her grandmother, sitting in a stiff wooden chair on the porch of her house in North Carolina where she went for a few weeks in summer. It was the room of a sixteen-year old girl, the kind of room that haunted the night time imaginings of teenage boys.

She dropped her book bag down onto the bed and glanced at the machine— no messages—and went into the kitchen where her mother sat, silently reading a letter.

"Hi, Ivy." she said without looking up. "It's from grandma. She's not doing too well at the moment." She paused. "How was school?"

"Fine. I got an A on the math test. What's wrong with Grandma? And why are you home so early?"

"They don't know, really. Something about her heart. It's not moving her blood around fast enough—that's how she explained it, anyway. And I'm not feeling too great myself, so I thought I'd come home and rest." Her mother looked beautiful in the late afternoon light—a few gray hairs, but her skin was smooth, the color of cocoa, and it was from her mother that she had inherited her beautiful eyes. She folded the letter up and put it back in the envelope.

"When's dad getting home?"

"Late. He's on duty. He said he'd call you later."

"Alright," Ivy said, and just then she heard the familiar sound of her telephone ring, and ran to get it.

"Hi, Yvonne." But it wasn't Yvonne who spoke.

"Hey, Ivy," the voice said, a boy's. "How you doing?"

"Fine, but who are you?"

"You can't tell?"

"No, I can't, so you better tell me. I don't play phone games."

"Herman."

"Who?"

"Herman, come on. You know me. We were talking yesterday—remember, out in front of the school."

"I remember," Ivy said, "but I don't remember handing out my phone number."

"You didn't. Your girl Yvonne gave it to me." Then it all swam dimly back into focus. On their way out of school the day before they had stopped to talk to a couple boys who always seemed to be standing there. Afterwards, as they walked to the subway, Ivy made the mistake of telling Yvonne she thought one of them was kind of cute.

"Yvonne said it would be alright if I called you."

"That was nice of her, but I don't even know you."

"That's why I called."

"Well, I don't talk on the phone to people I don't know, alright? My mother doesn't allow it."

"Don't tell her, then."

"I also don't lie, and I don't hang up on people, so you better say goodbye."

"Alright, but don't forget—it's Herman," he said. He had a soft, and pleasant face, she remembered, but she had no particular interest in talking to him, especially with her mother hovering around, listening.

"Goodbye." Ivy said, trying to sound mad, and hung up.

"Who was that?" her mother asked, sticking her head into the room.

"A friend," Ivy said.

"Didn't sound like just a friend to me, Ivy. I don't want strangers calling you in this house."

"He's not a stranger—just a stupid boy."

"You're only sixteen."

"Only? Anyway, I told him not to be calling here anymore—Yvonne gave him my number."

"That was nice of her."

Her mother walked backed to the kitchen, and Ivy knew better than to pursue this line of discussion. Instead, she quickly dialed Yvonne's number—busy, as usual.

"I'm going to kill you, Yvonne," she said later, when she finally got her on the phone, she cussed her out and made her promise never to give out her number again. Yvonne just laughed.

The next morning when she came into homeroom, Ivy walked past the tall, thin kid she had seen the day before, down at the pit with that weird, bearded guy.

"You shouldn't smoke." she said to Zak as she walked by him, but by the time he heard her and looked she was already halfway across the room.

"I didn't inhale," Zak said after her, and Ivy rolled her eyes and sat down across from Yvonne. "Yeah, right—just like Clinton." He wanted to say something else to her, to keep the ball rolling, but she had already turned to Yvonne.

"What did you say to *him*?" Yvonne wanted to know.

"Nothing." Ivy said. "I'm not talking to you, remember?"

"Oh, yeah," Yvonne said. "You don't like talking to boys, either, do you?"

"Not really."

"I can see." Yvonne said, sucking her teeth, and added to herself. "A White boy, too."

"What?" Ivy asked her, but she was already gone.

Seven Minutes

It was almost the end of the quarter and Zak wasn't doing very well in U.S. History: the Revolution, Indians, various declarations and battles and constitutional conventions, all swirled around in his head in a dull, confusing jumble. The teacher, Mr. Carey, was a large, friendly man, a specialist in history and basketball. He had been at the school ever since he had graduated from college, four years after having graduated from Central himself, the story went, and came back as a teacher and assistant basketball coach; he had to wait ten years before his predecessor finally died and he realized his real life long ambition of becoming head coach.

Second period was French, and the teacher was a beautiful, young woman on a one-year teacher exchange, who had swapped places with a plump and dour middle-aged teacher named Ms. Probert, who had thick ankles and was shaped like a pear.

"Those poor French kids," joked Peter Zorn on the first day of class. "They got the raw end of that deal." Mme. Maillard had jet black hair and a pretty, pale face with lips that always seemed to Zak a different shade of red. Her lips formed an almost perfect "O" formed by years of perfect enunciation, though the ruder boys had other theories to its origins as well. She always wore pants, and her waist was thin, and her ass was the shape of a full and perfect heart, upside down. She walked around the room alot on the theory that watching someone moving kept the students awake which, in her own case, was true: all eyes followed her as she drifted around the room, asking students to conjugate "avoir", or "faire", or "désir", with a light, gentle tap on the shoulder, or a glance from her wide, brown eyes, her eyebrows raised in expectation. She was hard, but fair, and by the second quarter French had become, for the first time that anyone could remember, one of the more popular subjects in the school.

Zak had the feeling she liked him—at least as well as anyone else, and when he studied at night it was generally with the vision of Mme. Maillard, gliding quietly past him, up the aisle, brushing his elbow with her hip, leaving

21

in her wake the faint trail of French perfume. He sometimes wondered if she brushed past him so close, touching him, on purpose.

By the end of the first quarter he had earned for himself a collection of B's and C's, with a B+ from Mme. Maillard, one of the highest grades in the class. From Mr. Carey, he had been awarded a straight C, a "Cat," Nick called it, which was better than the "Dog" that he got. "Capitalist Pig." Nick muttered.

Zak's mother was not overly impressed with his grades. "You better try harder next semester, if you want to go to a fancy college." His mother had said.

"Oh, you mean like Princeton, like Dad—no/thanks. I hate that place." Zak said, then added. "Don't worry, I'm still getting adjusted."

"I know. Just don't wait too long. Eleventh grade is important for college."

"Well, maybe if I was still back home at Olney I'd be doing better."

"Maybe so, but we're not. If you don't like it here, by spring, you can go back and live with your father." Lately, she had started to refer to his father not as "Pete," or "Dad," as she always had, but as "your father," as if he were someone she was no longer related to. "Maybe we'll both go back," Zak said, "and get out of this shit city."

His mother sighed. She was standing at the kitchen sink doing dishes; she looked tired. Ever since they had gotten there she worked half time at the University, then went to classes, and then did her school work at the kitchen table until long after Zak had gone to bed. "When I graduate, but that's another two years off. I have to do something for myself," she said.

"Yeah, me too," Zak said, not knowing, exactly, what he meant. His mother looked over at him suspiciously. "Like what?" she said.

"Like studying more."

"Good idea."

"I know, mom. I think I might be getting adjusted soon."

"Well, we both have to keep working at it. Life isn't always easy."

"Actually, it's not that bad. I kind of like the school."

"I'm glad. Now I better go do some work."

But if truth be known, Zak's favorite class was homeroom: the only problem was it was only seven minutes long. The other problem was that, although he now and then managed to say a few words to this girl named Ivy, and one day asked her a few questions about what colleges she was thinking of applying to, most of the time he could barely say hello. She usually came in at the last minute and sat with Yvonne, who had laid her enormous leather coat across the empty chair next to her. Then Zak would just sit and, trying not to be too obvious about it, watch her as she talked—her beautiful eyes, her light brown skin, the converging lines of her lips that reminded him of the statues he had seen once in the museum, from Egypt. Her eyes were brown, but one of them, it sometimes seemed to Zak, was slightly lighter shade than the other, or was it just the way the early morning sunlight fell across her face? Sometimes she wore pants, other times skirts but usually a sweater made, it seemed to Zak, from the softest kind of wool, shaved from the bellies of new born lambs, high in the mountains of Peru. Or were there llamas in Peru?

That's how Zak spent the first seven minutes of almost every day, trying not to stare, trying to think of things to say to her when the period ended, but it never happened. She was guarded closely by Yvonne, and they usually left in a hurry, disappearing for the day. Now and then, if he was lucky, he would catch a glimpse of her somewhere, the flash of her face in the cafeteria, a sudden sense of her in the hallway, and there she would be, a bundle of books clasped to her chest, glancing up at him, saying "Hi" and then passing quickly away. One day after school, he saw her standing by "the wall," where kids hung around after school, with Yvonne and a bunch of boys, among them Herman Jones.

"Hey, Hayseed," Herman said when he saw him. "Hey, Herman. How are you doing?" Zak said. He could feel Ivy looking up at him, and he managed to slow down and say, "Hi Ivy." He was about to stop, but then what? "Hi." he thought he heard Ivy say back, but he wasn't sure, so he kept walking, like a fool, scuffling his feet through the leaves.

Genes

"Genetics," her father said one evening before dinner, as he scanned the paper. Somehow, they had gotten onto the subject of beauty, why some people had it and others didn't. "It's all a matter of genetics. But we have no say in these matters. It's all random—to a point. Now, if you had come out a shade or two lighter, I might have started to worry." He glanced at his wife, but she did not humor him. "You're beautiful, and my daughter," he continued, "and that's all that matters."

All of her life, people had been telling her this, that she was beautiful: Ivy, with the *good* hair; Ivy with the brown almond eyes; Ivy, with skin the color of sunlight turned brown by the summer sun; Ivy, the girl with the slight and lovely body, swelling into that of a woman.

"Stay out of the sun," one of her aunts down in North Carolina was fond of saying. "It will ruin your color. You don't want to be dark like us, do you?"

"Why not?" she wanted to answer, but never did. Even her friends seemed to sometimes envy her for her complexion, and seemed to think she had it made because of it; for her part, Ivy sometimes secretly envied the deep, rich brown of her father's skin, or Yvonne's, closer to chocolate that caramel.

Herman Jones told her she was "fine" when she talked to him on the phone in the evenings; her mother didn't want her talking on the phone while she was trying to do homework, but she had figured out a way to turn off the ringer and listen when the answering machine clicked on, then talked softly, with the radio on, hanging up quickly when she heard her mother's footstep in the hall. In any case, after his first phone call Ivy had taken more notice of Herman at school, and stopped to talk to him and his friends, sometimes, as they stood by the wall. Yvonne liked to ask her when she was going to "get with" Herman finally, to which she would generally respond, "Not soon."

"Why not? He's cute."

"So? If you don't mind, I'd like to graduate from High school without having a baby, or a fatal illness."

Yvonne laughed. "That's what raincoats are for."

"*Raincoats*—cute. Thanks for the tip—I took 'Know your body' in seventh grade, too, remember?"

"Anyway, kids don't get that disease, hardly."

"They don't? Do you ever read the papers?" Ivy said.

"Not much, but that doesn't mean I have to live like a nun."

At this point, Ivy decided not to answer. Some arguments were not worth getting into, especially with Yvonne. She had once asked Ivy in a half accusatory way, if she was "still" a virgin, and against her better judgment Ivy had said, "None of your business." To which Yvonne had responded, "I thought so."

In truth, she had kissed only once, but that was with a boy down in South Carolina, where Ivy went in the summers to visit her grandmother. It was hot, and they were in a field, somewhere, in the shade of a chestnut tree, and a warm wind was blowing through the branches. They were just standing there when one of his hands settled on the small of her back, and another reached up and wrapped itself into her long, soft hair, and the next thing she knew his lips were pressed against hers, and her new breasts were held against the smooth muscles of his chest. They kissed, there, in the cool, blue shadows of the tree, and when he had suggested they sit down for a while, pointing to a matted place in the grass, Ivy had taken back her breath, shook her head, and they had walked home. A week later, she had returned to school, and he had written her several letters, and she had written back, but as the autumn wore on, and the bright yellows and oranges of October gave way to gray and silver and brown, the letters had slowed down, and then stopped altogether. But the memory of this kiss remained, and as Ivy lay in her bed at night, among her teddy bears and pillows, with the lacy shadows of leaves swaying on the wall, listening to the love songs that flooded in over the radio, she sometimes thought of this kiss, the warmth of his skin, and the way her body seemed to glow, giving off heat as they pressed against him. She would touch the swelling contours of herself, and looked forward to the spring when she would go down south to stay with her grandmother again, imagined lying down on that matted place in the grass with him, wondering what it would feel like, that first time, wanting to know.

But somehow, she couldn't transfer what she felt for him onto Herman Jones, didn't feel like kissing him, or going out, or doing any of the things that Yvonne liked to talk about. Odder still, when she thought about boys, she sometimes thought about that tall, shy boy from homeroom who often seemed to be staring at her, or gazing into the air around her, and when she passed behind him on the way into class, he seemed to glance up at her as if he was about to speak and then didn't. She almost wanted to laugh, sometimes, at his shyness, and say something just so he would feel better. He had straight and light brown hair, a mild face, with a few freckles, and soft gray eyes that sometimes, in a certain light, looked blue, or blue green, the way the color of the sea changes before a storm.

He wasn't a nerd, or a geek, or a preppie—didn't seem to hang out with any crowd. He did spend a lot of time with that tall, thin kid with the beard, and she had heard Herman Jones call him as Hayseed. But she, too, was shy, and Yvonne was always saving her seat, and if she ever tried to change hers, it would be Yvonne she would have to listen to. And Yvonne, she happened to know, didn't believe in crossing over.

"I wasn't brought up that way." Ivy said.

"How were you brought up, then? To love White people, after they stole us from Africa, and brought us here?"

"No, but not to be scared of them, either."

"Who's scared? I'm just not giving it up for them, that's all. Plus, I'm not having any mixed babies. That's whack."

"Come on, Yvonne," Ivy said. "Why are you always talking about babies? Are you planning something? And anyway, this isn't supposed to matter anymore. Get over it."

Yvonne laughed. "I'll get over it when they stop following me around stores, thinking I'm going to steal something." It was true: more than once Ivy had been with Yvonne and the salesgirl kept following them around, asking them if they needed anything?

Ivy couldn't think of a response and let it go; after that, she tried to avoid the topic. She had better things to worry about, like getting good grades and trying to enjoy her last couple years of school before her real life would begin. When that would be, what it would be like, she could hardly imagine.

Chill

A week after Thanksgiving it snowed—a sudden, unexpected fall that had the forecasters baffled, and gave Zak, walking to school the following morning, a deep stab of nostalgia, wishing he was back home where it really snowed—one foot, or two, not these slight, urban dustings that melted the next day. The snow made him miss Vermont, his father, the life they used to have there. Though he spoke with his father every week, he hadn't seen him since one weekend in late September when he went home to hang out with his friends. But Thanksgiving had been alright—a couple of his mother's friends came over, and a great aunt he had hardly ever known before, and afterwards he and Nick walked down by the river and smoked a couple of cigarettes, and drank a beer Nick had smuggled out of his parents' house. Afterwards, they walked along the river, then up the square to the pit, and hung around in the cold, November air until it got dark and they wandered home.

But it was beautiful in the park outside of school—everything turned to white, silver plumes of steam floating out from the mouths of the laughing, jostling, students, throwing fistfuls of snow and trying to knock each other down. It was the first day of the new quarter, and he was vaguely nervous about his new classes: French, US History with old man Carey, Biology, Math; he needed a fifth course, an elective of some sort, but had no idea of what to take, and should have figured it out by now, and would have to go see his advisor—his French teacher, Mme. Maillard.

"You should have done all this before, of course." she said, as he sat down in her office. She was in a rush.

"Yeah," Zak admitted. "I just got too busy at the end of last semester."

"I see," she said, putting on her glasses, and looking down at Zak's crumpled course schedule, three credits short. She was wearing black pants, very tight as usual, and a white shirt with its top two buttons left undone, so, from a certain angle he could see the lacy fringe of her bra, and the creamy white swelling of her breast. Her eyes were soft and brown, her cheeks, he could see up close, lightly touched with freckles. Sitting so close he felt surrounded by the scent of her perfume.

"Et le problème," she began, "is that these courses are already full. Comprenez-vous?"

"Yes—I mean, oui." Zak said, vaguely embarrassed. "Et la seule classe ouverte est black studies. Vous connaissez Mme. Newman?"

"No," Zak said. "I mean *non.*"

"This is good for you?"

"Um, well. I don't know anything about it."

"Very good, then—you *do* need it." She wrote something down on the sheet of paper.

"Prenez cette papier a` la première classe—aujourd hui." She instructed him.

"*Anyone* can take this class?"

For the first time, she looked at him with her soft brown eyes. "Mais oui! L'instruction est pour tous. Don't be foolish. And next time, do it earlier; ça va? Bonne chance." she said, and stood up to leave, so that her lap, swathed in cloth, was about half a foot from his face. "Let me know how it goes, okay? In the meantime, study your French? You have a small talent in this."

"Gee, thanks." Zak said, and would have sat there, looking at her all day had she not said, "Oui, j'ai une reunion stupide, maintenant. Je dois partir," She swayed out of the room in her black pants, heels of her black shoes clicking as she went.

Orvella Newman was a short, good looking woman in her late thirties or so with dreds, wire rim glasses, and a slight southern drawl. Now and then she would slip into the phrases of her native Georgia, like "Y'all", and her students would joke, and call her "Y'all Newman." But mostly they called her "Orvella", or "Ms. Newman."

"Not Mrs., or Miss, please." she said on the first day of the new quarter. "Orvella is fine. Or Maliaka, if you want—that's my Swahili name, from when I lived in Tanzania." She favored lipstick in red, or none at all, and wore clothes of an African looking print, and a kente cloth scarf draped around her neck. She attracted a loyal following at the school, not only because she was one of the few Black teachers but because she was young and smart and offered one of the only two courses in "Black Studies"; in fact it was she who had gotten them approved by the school board several years before.

"Alright," she was now saying, standing in front of the twelve or thirteen students who had come on the first day of class. "Welcome."

"Thank you," a few students said back.

"Thank you," she said. "I hope you enjoy the class, and get something out it."

The students didn't sit in rows, like in most of their other classes, but in a loose circle of desks, so that no one could hide. "I like to see everyone's shoes and faces." Ms. Newman said. "This is a discussion-oriented class, and you have to come here with an open mind, willing to think and discuss. And you have to do the reading; if you don't, it will be rather obvious, and you'll have to drop the class—or fail, it's up to you. Is that clear?" A few people nodded.

"And one more thing," Ms. Newman said. "This is not, contrary to popular mythology, a 'Black' class. It's a class for everyone, is about something that everyone needs to know about, and is generally not taught at most schools. We are going to read some important books, and discuss some of the issues they raise, but we're not here to whine about White folks, so if that is your main motivation, you might think twice."

Ivy looked around, to see what kind of reaction she was getting. A homeboy boy in the back raised his hand; he was sitting sideways in seat and had a baseball hat on sideways. It was Harold Pierce, one of the kids who hung around with Herman after school.

"Yes, young man?" Orvella asked him.

"Yeah, but we can say what we want in here, can't we?"

"What do you mean?"

"You know, like, say what we *really* think."

"Of course you can say what you really think. As long as you can back it up with facts, not myths. And you'll have to write weekly, one page response papers—a kind of dialogue with me. You write me; I write back. Alright?"

"I guess," he said, shrugging. "As long as we can express ourselves."

"You can express yourselves all day long, as long as you have something to say. And, ah, we don't allow hats here."

Harold sighed and if you were sitting near him, you might have heard him mutter "Shit," as he slowly took off his hat.

"And if you swear again, you'll be out for the semester." she added casually.

Ivy enjoyed this little exchange, and was glad Ms. Newman was getting the upper hand, establishing supremacy. So many of the White teachers—especially the so-called "liberal ones"—let these kids get over on them, like they were scared to tell them to stop acting like assholes. She instinctively liked her, and had waited since freshman year to get into her class.

"Any more questions?" she asked.

Ivy raised her hand.

"Yes, Ms. Whitman?" How did she know her name?

"Hmm, can you tell us some of the books we'll be reading?"

"Yes," she said, "thank you," She took from her desk a pile of syllabi, and passed them out. It was four pages long.

"I like to spell things out from the beginning," she said. "So if you will kindly read this over carefully, we can go over the particulars tomorrow. In the meantime, please pick up a copy of the Frederick Douglas book at the annex, and read the first thirty pages, or so."

"Thirty?"

"Or forty, if you want," she said, smiling, and that's when Whitney Houston started singing one of her corny songs that grownups thought kids liked, and everyone got up and started to leave. Ivy gathered up her books.

"I'm glad to see you, Ivy," Ms. Newman said on their way out. "I've heard good things about you."

"Thanks." Ivy said, "It seems like a great class."

"Well—I hope so." Ms. Newman said, and they were about to go out into the hall together when they were met, at the door, by a tall, thin kid, panting slightly, and holding a slip paper the same shade of pink of his face. Ivy smiled at the sight of Zak. "A bit late, aren't you?"

"Only a little." he said and then turned to Ms. Newman.

"Sorry I'm late, Mrs. Newman, but . . ."

"Ms." she said. "And class just ended. Bring that pink slip tomorrow, if you still want to get in. And ask Miss Whitman what you missed, *if* she has the time."

"Alright," Zak said, then watched her as she walked away. "Shit," he muttered to himself, then said to Ivy, "Maybe you can tell me tomorrow, in homeroom?"

"That's fine." Ivy said, and smiled. "What happened, you got lost?"

"Ah, sort of." Zak said.

"Well, I'll tell you tomorrow. Don't worry. She's cool." Ivy said, and then left.

Someone came up behind him and thumped him on the back. He turned quickly to see Nick's bearded, ghoulish face.

"Yo, Zakster. What's up? Let's go have a smoke? I've got a free period."

"Me, too," Zak said. "Let's get out of here. I think I'm fucking up."

"Naw, you're straight." Nick said. "Just chill—everything's cool."

"Whatever you say, mountain man."

Pure

Every day for several weeks now, Ivy would emerge from the doors of the school to find Herman sitting on the wall, waiting for her, and today was no different. Some days she would be with Yvonne, and they would stop and talk, but Yvonne hadn't been in school today. She didn't really feel like talking, felt like getting home to her robin's egg room and her telephone and books, but couldn't afford to get a reputation as a snob; besides, he called her almost every night anyway.

"Hey, Ivy," he said. "What's up?"

"The sun, the moon, the stars. Plus, I have to go—I have a paper due tomorrow." This wasn't exactly true; it was due the following week.

"You can't chill for a while?"

"Not really."

"Let me walk you, then. I have a few minutes before practice."

"If you want." Ivy shrugged.

"I want," he said, and nodded to his friends, and they nodded back; lately, Herman had begun to act like they were a couple, or something, though more than once, in more than one way, she had told him this wasn't in the cards.

It was December already, but a strange and sudden warm spell had come, and the campus of the college they crossed on their way home was filled with students—playing frisbee, hanging out, sitting on the steps. They didn't really look like genius material—just ordinary kids, only older. Herman was talking about his classes, and how some teacher was threatening to flunk him and knock him off the basketball team.

"Well, if you don't do the work," Ivy said, "What do you expect?"

"I am doing the work. He just doesn't like me because I sit in the back with my boys."

"You're probably talking and acting out."

"Not you, too?" Herman said, stopping in front of the enormous stone steps of the Library, rising up beside them in a slope of granite and stone.

"You're beginning to sound like the teachers, like some of those goody two shoes, always kissing butt."

"God, can you cut it out? All I said was, if you don't do the work, if you don't try, you can't expect to pass. Not everyone's like Mr. Cary—mess up all semester, and then go sit with him for an hour and talk about basketball and everything's fine again. Some teachers don't care if you're Mr. Basketball."

"And what about you? Do you care?"

"If that's what you like, that's what you're good at. But you have to study, too, if you want to do anything afterwards. You can't play basketball your whole life, chances are, you're not going to make it to the NBA, so you better have a plan B."

"Says who?"

"Statistics. Plus, you're only about five feet eight, on a day with low gravity waves."

"Five nine, and counting. And look at Spud Web. Anyway, when are you coming to a game?"

"When I get no homework."

"Yvonne's trying out to be a cheerleader. Why don't you?"

"I don't look good with pom-poms, jumping around smiling in a plaid skirt. Besides," she added, glancing behind her, "I don't have the right body type."

"I wouldn't know about that," Herman said, running up and down her body with his eyes. "Looks fine to me. Anyway, we need some more Black girls. Sonia's the only one, but she's really Spanish. How do you think we feel, playing with all those White chicks cheering us on?"

"Probably like you've died and gone to heaven." What was it about Herman that brought out her mean streak?

He had inched closer to her, so she could feel his warm, hopeful body pressing toward hers, and feel one of his hands take hold of her lapel, looking for a hand to hold; hers were happy where they were, in her pockets.

"Hey, it's just hands," he had said. "Relax."

"I am relaxed," Ivy said. "And I want to keep it that way."

"I thought we were going out," Herman said.

"Really?" Ivy said. "Where do you get your information? Ask them again."

Herman just shook his head, turned away, and looked across the campus. "Yvonne told me you were kind of rough, but I didn't know it was this bad."

"Look, Herman, we're friends, right? That's all I can handle right now. If you need more than that, maybe I'm not the right person for you to be walking home every day. There's plenty of girls who like you. I'm sure they don't mind holding hands, etc . . ."

"Etc . . ." Herman chuckled. "Yeah, but it's you I want, and my boys are laughing at me 'cause you don't give me any."

"Maybe you need some new boys, then. Or call one of your cheerleaders. Look, I'm not interested in a boyfriend right now. I have enough to worry about."

"Like keeping yourself *pure*?"

Whatever hope Herman had with Ivy went up in smoke and out the window. She blushed, and turned.

"Joke." he said, but knew it was no use, and watched her as she walked away. He knew better than to follow. So that's what they thought of her—she was "pure"—a cold, frigid virgin who wouldn't give it up: the word was out. Why couldn't she be like Yvonne and her friends—willing and able to oblige these pretty, long lashed, smooth talking boys with beepers and money to buy them clothes with? They were tough looking and talking, said *fuck* and *bitch* and *nigger* a lot, but when you got to know them, soft, actually, and shy— unless you got pregnant, that is, and suddenly they weren't sure if it was "theirs" or not, and they went back to their friends.

But if her father caught her with a boy at home he'd have to jump out the window or fight—"wished he joined the army, before I got through with him." But she had no desire to bring him home, or to let him kiss her, or let him hold his taut, needy body against hers. But she was tired of hearing Yvonne say, in her nightly telephone calls, "What are you waiting for—marriage?"

Although it wasn't exactly warm, it wasn't cold outside, either, and there were lots of kids in the pit—scraggly boys with leather coats, pale girls in baggy corduroys, with earrings in their belly buttons. She wanted to sit for a minute and watch, but who would she talk to? She slowed down and pretended she was looking around for someone, as if they had a meeting planned or something. That's when she saw them—the weird kid with the beard, and his trusty sidekick from homeroom that, at that exact moment, looked up and saw her. Zak waved and stood up, so she walked over to them.

"Ivy, I presume," he said, smiling his shy, curious smile.

"You presume correctly. Smoking again?"

"Nah, I quit. It's bad for you, I heard." Behind him, Nick just sat there, tugging on his beard. Ivy realized she didn't even know his real name.

"Can I ask you something?" Zak said.

"You just did." she said, and then added, "Go ahead—ask another one. But me first—what's your real name, besides Haystack, or whatever they call you?"

"Zak, or Zachary, if you want to be formal. And this is my trusty sidekick, friend, Nick, the bearded wonder."

"Nick I know," Ivy said. "We took math together once."

"I'm flattered you remembered." Nick muttered behind him, glanced toward Ivy, then resumed gazing into the distance.

"I think I'm in trouble," Zak said.

"With the police?"

"No, our new teacher."

"No you're not, but it might help if you came at the beginning of class, not at the end."

"I was late, and I didn't want to walk in the middle, so I stood outside like a fool and waited for the class to be over."

"You're right, that was foolish. Next time, come in late, and look sorry."

"Good idea."

"But she's fine. Serious, but nice."

"Beside, some kids might not want me in there, anyway."

"Ah . . ." Ivy said, rolling her eyes, "The truth comes out. No, she already gave a speech about that—everybody's welcome. The more the merrier, Black, White, other. She already told us—it's not a class for complaining about White folks."

Zak watched her face, and wondered if he had just made a fool of himself, revealed something about him he would have preferred remained hidden. He wanted to say something else, but he got distracted looking at her long eyelashes, the stray strands of hair that had escaped from her blue hair band and hung above her eyes, glinting in the late afternoon sun—shades of yellow, orange, brown.

"I'll show you my syllabus in homeroom tomorrow. I don't have it with me now."

"Cool," Zak said.

"Don't be scared, she won't bite." He might have thought she was making fun of him if she hadn't smiled at him, then turned, said "See you tomorrow," and he stood there like an imbecile and watched her leave.

"Smooth, Hayboy," Nick said behind him. "Pretty smooth. Who said you country boys can't talk with girls."

"Shit," Zak said. "I'm just trying to find out about this class."

"Relax, it's a free country, more or less. Besides, you might even learn something."

"That would be nice."

"Tell me about it," Nick said, taking a drag on his cigarette, and then blew a blue cloud of smoke out into the cold, winter air. "She's cute," Nick conceded, snapping a cigarette out of his pack and sparking up. "Smart, too. But she's still a girl. Her friend Yvonne—now, there's a *real* woman for you."

"Oh, yeah," Zak said. "Like *you* would know."

"I *know*, don't worry." Nick said, tugging thoughtfully on his wispy yellow beard. "It doesn't matter much, anyway. We're both dreaming."

"What do you mean?"

"What do I mean? They wouldn't even look at us. They don't date White boys, that's all."

"Says who?"

"Common knowledge, Zakster—welcome to America. It's nothing personal, it's just not cool. The brothers wouldn't like it."

"What brothers?" Zak said, and Nick rolled his eyes.

"Don't they teach you anything up in the woods—the *brothers*, man. The Black dudes—they don't want their women hanging with us White boys."

"Why's that?"

"Just because, man—we're the enemy. It all goes back to history. Sometimes I forget you just got here—like she says in the Wizard of Oz, 'I don't think we're in Kansas anymore.'"

"Thanks for the tip, tin man." Zak said, irked by this new bit of information.

"No problem, scarecrow."

Ivy still didn't feel like going home, much, and wouldn't have minded sitting down, for a minute, with these two oddballs—the one with the wispy beard, and the other, tall one, with a smooth, innocent face and shy, blue eyes that always seemed to be staring at her. He made her want to laugh, for some reason: he seemed so naïve, but confident, like he was always thinking something, but never said it.

What did she know about White boys? The usual myths: they can't jump; can't dance (true); didn't know how to "do it"—as if she would know. They had small you know whats, of course; "went down" on women, supposedly, unlike Black boys, who said it was nasty, dirty, wrong. Who really knew, anyway—everyone said Black girls were "easy", too, and Ivy was living proof that this wasn't always true.

She stood on the subway platform, listening to a blind man playing a guitar—some pitiful, sad song she seemed to remember from somewhere. Yvonne would be calling her to see if she was going to some dance or other, at school. The blind man finished his song and Ivy dropped a quarter into his hat. He heard it clink, and said "Thank you" to the darkness.

A soft, stale wind swept down the subway platform, gathering force, and a moment later the train pushed in behind it, but instead of getting on Ivy sat down on the bench and listened to another song—one train, two trains three; there was something strange and pleasant about sitting here, about not getting on, like she was homeless or something. Some boys from school came by and tried to talk to her, laughing and muttering something about her legs, but when she wouldn't respond they moved on, cackling their way down the platform. "She thinks she's all that," she thought she heard one of them say, shuffling away. That was what some of them thought about her—she was a snob because she did well in school, and didn't curse or talk bad or go out with boys on the weekends. Once, when she was in fifth grade some kids had accused her of "acting White," and made up a little song about her name, something about "Little Ivy White girl, sitting on a tree . . ." She had been hurt and cried, and when she went home and told her parents her mother just shook her head, and said, "Ivy, there are just some people who don't want to see anyone succeed, and they want to drag everyone else down. So you just keep doing your work and don't worry about them, or else they'll pull you down with them, like crabs in a barrel." And as her mother had looked at her with eyes that were suddenly filled with a strange, unexpected sadness, she seemed to Ivy her mother was the prettiest woman in the world. Jostled by the memory, she boarded the next train and went home.

Planting Time

"What are you reading?" Zak's mother asked him, walking into the room. He was sitting on the couch with his tattered book, with the television on, but the sound off.

"The Frederick Douglass dude."

"Cool dude—how is it?"

"Page one is great, I don't know about the rest of it."

"Why don't you turn the television off?"

"It helps me concentrate—I'm one of the television generation, remember? It's our drug."

"Well, we don't do drugs, here." She said, and turned off the TV.

Zak looked up and said, "What are we doing for Christmas?"

"What do you want to do?"

"Go back to Vermont, I guess. But not for the whole time."

"No, why not?"

"I don't know. I'm trying to make friends here."

"What about your Vermont friends?"

"I'll see them—go skiing, probably." He wanted to ask her where *she* would stay, if they were going back to their old house like before, if they were going to move back in with his father.

"And what about you?" he asked.

"What about me?"

"Are you coming, too?"

"Of course—why wouldn't I?"

"Well, you and Dad don't exactly seem like the perfect couple these days." With that, she sat heavily down on the couch beside him.

"That's true," she said. "We're not having the easiest time, right now. But we're trying to work it out. And the best thing for me to do is to try and do something for myself. Your father's a nice man, but he never really thought I should have a life of my own, a career. And this is something I can't exactly do in Vermont. They don't have graduate schools for education in Brattleboro.

And we both—we all—thought coming to the city for a year or two would be good for you. There's more to the world than Vermont, as nice as it is." She paused. "Well, I hope you tell me what you learn in that class. It seems interesting."

"Oh, I will, Mom. Every week I'll give you an oral report."

"Teenagers," she said, smiled, and left the room.

As he read, his mind kept drifting back to Ivy, the girl with long eyelashes and beautiful eyes. She seemed to be amused by him, but he couldn't get her to sit still long enough to talk to her. The day before, the first full day of Black Studies, he had left his coat on the seat beside him, in the hopes that she would come in late and have to sit beside him, but then miss dreadlocks had come in, and said, "May I sit here, please?" Then he wondered how it looked— the only two white kids sitting together, like they were friends or something. He went back to his book:

> I was born in Tuckahoe, near Hillsborough, and about twelve miles from Easton, in Talbot County, Maryland. I have no accurate knowledge of my age, never having seen any authentic record containing it. By far the larger part of slaves know as little of their ages as horses know of theirs, and it is the wish of most masters within my knowledge to keep their slaves thus ignorant. I do not remember to have ever met a slave who could tell of his birthday. They seldom come nearer to it than planting-time, harvest-time, cherry-time, spring-time, or fall-time.

At this same moment, Ivy was trying to do her own homework, but the phone kept ringing: first it was Yvonne, just talking; then it was Marianna, a girl from her math class who was flunking out and had latched on to Ivy as a kind of life raft—a last ditch attempt to save herself. Then it was Herman, who left her a message saying he was sorry, and he didn't care about "all that", and just wanted to be friends. He also wanted to know if she wanted to go to the dance with him. Then there was another message from Yvonne: "Ivy, you nerd. Stop studying so much. Call me. Herman says you aren't being very nice to him, but he wants to take you to the dance, anyway. But we have to make plans and figure out which after party to go to. Call me."

Herman, Ivy thought, getting angry; and this time, she turned the ringer off and disconnected the machine. Why was Herman calling Yvonne every five minutes reporting? "Shit," Ivy said to herself, but softly, enjoying the sound of the word.

That's when she heard a light knocking at the door.

"Come in," she said, and her mother pushed open the door. "Now what are you cursing about?" she asked. Her mother had good ears.

"Oh, nothing—just Yvonne, and Herman, leaving me stupid messages."

"That makes you curse?"

"Can't I have any privacy around here? I thought I was alone."

"You were. I was just walking by."

"Really? With your ear pressed to the door?"

"I did not." Her mother said, softening. "Anyway, don't let these friends of yours throw you off track. Just keep up your good work, and everything will work out."

"You think so, mom?"

"Yes, I do."

"Why, are you worried about something?"

"Not really. I just get tired of being Miss goody two shoes—everyone thinking I'm a nerd, and they think I think I'm all that, and . . ."

"Who thinks that?"

"Yvonne, and her crowd, for starters."

"Well, you have your life, they have theirs—you see where she is in ten years. If you're looking for advice, I wouldn't go running to her."

"I know—she's just a pain in the butt, sometime."

"Yes, I know. So is her mother. The apple doesn't fall far from the tree. But don't you worry about it. Do some work before dinner, if you can. And it might be easier if you're not in bed."

"I love my bed," Ivy said, as her mother closed the door behind her. Then she picked up her book, and pulled the covers up around her chin, and settled into the cocoon of her room, a safe kingdom of pink and blue. She sometimes wondered if she was going to be the last, teenage virgin in America.

Graffiti

One morning in mid-December, a week before Christmas vacation, the first girl who entered the girl's bathroom on the third floor discovered some strange words written on the white tiles with black spray paint: there was a swastika or two, and then, "Death to queers, Niggers, Spics—White People rule!!"

"Oh, shit," said Colleen Stamps, a rather plain, pale girl with braces and a C minus average, quickly taking the lit cigarette she had gone in to smoke and throwing it into the toilet, flushing, clearing the smoke with frantic waving of her arms; and then she went out into the hall to call her friends. "Hey, you guys. Look at this bad shit in here!!" And in they went.

"Oh my God!!" one girl said, "That's nasty." Another laughed nervously. Colleen Stamps ran to the office, and the assistant vice principal came striding in to see, and soon no one was allowed in the girls bathroom except for Mr. Zorn, the art teacher, who was summoned to take a photograph, and then the janitor, Mr. Zachary, a soft spoken man who kept talking to himself as he scrubbed the walls with toxic chemicals. "I don't know about all this," he kept muttering to himself. "I don't know. I grew up in Mississippi, and I thought we'd left all this behind us, and then, to come up here, and find it here, well, that's distressing . . ."

All day, rumors flew around the school as to what had actually been written on the walls, and Colleen Stamps, as the one who had actually discovered it, became, for the first time in her life, popular. But in all the excitement and blur of activity, she couldn't actually remember what was on the wall. She remembered the swastika, of course, and "Nigger", and "Spic" and "Queer", and something about "white people", but couldn't remember how they had all been put together. The Principal issued a statement saying that the high school would not tolerate such behavior, and wanted to speak with anyone who might know who had done it. They had never had this kind of problem, and weren't about to start now. Some students laughed, others hugged each other, others said, "I can't believe it; I don't believe it." Others dismissed it as the work of some demented "PWT" which, Zak learned soon enough, stood for "poor white trash," someone like his uncle Carl, he imagined, who lived in a rusty trailer at the end of a long, dirt road in Olney, his yard strewn with junk. A few student groups called meetings: the Hillel Society, the Black Students Union, the Latino Alliance. Then, on a tip from a student who had heard someone boasting about it in the bathroom, three boys were brought into the Principal's office—two white kids and a Dominican boy who was running in the same "crew", as they called themselves. They admitted to the crime, say they were only playing, and the next day suspended for two weeks, maybe expelled later.

"Alright," Ms. Newman said, a few days later. "If you don't have a book, sit next to someone who does. She was walking around the room, coming close to the desks, tapping on people's books with a pen. "But before we start, how do you feel about the term 'African American?'"

From where he was sitting, Zak had a good view of the room—the Heather dreadlocks, a wispy Spanish looking kid he recognized from U.S. History, a Somalian boy, the seven or eight others were Black. Ivy was a couple of seats down from him, but hidden, and he could see, only, her brown leather shoes.

"I'm not no African." Kevin Peters said, and the class laughed.

"No?" Ms Newman wanted to know. "Then where are you from?"

"Right here."

"And what about your parents?"

"New York."

"And what about their parents?"

"Down south somewhere."

"And how did they get there?"

"How do I know?"

"Well, you might want to think about it some time, if you have a moment. Or you could ask them. Why do you think some of us prefer the term 'African American' to 'Black?'" she asked, looking around.

"Yes, Ms. Coombs."

"Because it's, like, somewhere—a place where people came from. Just like European-Americans tells us where white people came from."

"Right—it refers to a continent. And for our purposes, in a class like this, it seems to me important that Black Americans came from somewhere—Africa."

A few people snickered. The boy in the back was shaking his head. "Maybe, but I'm still American, not African."

"That's true, but it is important to remember. Just as it is important for the Dutch and Italians and Chinese to remember where they came from—with one large difference. And what is it?"

Ivy raised her hand. "Yes, Ivy?"

"Africans weren't given a choice."

"Right," Ms. Newman said. "And that has affected everything, so to speak, that has happened in America up until today."

Zak was sitting off to the side, afraid to take his eyes off the teacher in case she called on him, but he knew where Ivy was, four seats over, and when she spoke he had looked over at her, without being too obvious about it. He was thinking about her shoes, and ankles when Ms. Newman said, "Good, a propos of current events in the school this week, our graffiti artists, I thought we could read from page 67. Does anyone want to read?"

For some reason Zak felt compelled to raise his hand, but soon wished he hadn't: it was the part of the Frederick Douglass book where his owner keeps telling his wife you can't teach a slave to read or write, because it will make them the unhappiest 'nigger' in the world. When he got to the word, he paused and then decided to spell it out: "If you give a n-i-g-g-e-r an inch he will take an ell. A n-i-g-g-e-r should know nothing but to obey his master—to do as he is told to do. Learning would spoil the best n-i-g-g-e-r in the world." People laughed when he spelled it out, and Ms. Newman thanked him for reading.

"That's nasty," someone said.

"Why is that?" Mrs. Newman asked. "If you walk around the hallways here, you hear it about thirty times a day and no one seems to mind."

"That's different. We don't use it like that. We use it, like, just to greet each other, you know, like, what's up, Dog?"

"Yes, but don't you think it's strange, that of all the words available in English language, this is the one that Black teenagers have chosen to call themselves?"

"It's different," someone else repeated.

"You're sure about that?"

"Yup."

"Well, you think about it, and listen to yourself and your friends, and decide if it's really how you want to name yourselves for the rest of your lives. And if you want to know where the word came from, just keep reading this book—it's right here."

"I'm still gonna use it." Jamaul said. "Those are my boys, my nigga's."

"And let me guess—you call your women friends your 'bitches' and 'hoes'?"

"I do," one girl said proudly, and everyone laughed.

"And is that what you want people to call your twelve year old sister?"

"It doesn't sound right, coming from you."

"Why not? What's good for the goose is good for the gander."

"Huh?" someone asked.

"I mean, if it works for you, why not me? And why—before the bell rings—does Mr. Auld tell his wife slaves shouldn't learn to read? Yes, Ivy?"

"Because they'll know too much."

"Right," Ms. Newman said. "Have you all heard the expression Ignorance is bliss?" She was walking between the desks, now. "The less the slaves knew, the better it was for their masters. The more information they had the more dangerous it was. If they could read, they would read maps, newpapers, the bible. Literacy becomes the most dangerous weapon against the masters."

"Yeah, but he fights, too," Tyrone said—"He beats the crap out of the overseer, and after that he doesn't lay a hand on him."

"That is true, too." she said. "He talks about literacy as a path to freedom, but he also has to fight back, physically, and that's when he said he really becomes a man. But he also says, at that point, he was willing to die, rather than be whipped. For a lot of people, this strategy didn't work—they got killed."

"Better dead than whipped." Tyrone said. "Nobody's gonna be whipping me."

"Fair enough."

Then the music started, Ms. Newman said, "Thank You. To be continued," and everyone shuffled out into the hall.

Smoke

"She's a sellout," Tyrone was saying, after school to Herman and Yvonne. "Trying to scare me, saying I'll end up dead. Shit. Any white guy calls me that and we'll see who ends up dead. Right, nigga?" Herman only half smiled. It was cold and still and gray, and as they talked their breath came out as clouds of silver. It was getting towards winter.

"Those kids who did it better find a new school. Man, I'll bust their brains. Yo . . ." he asked, trying to get some response out of Herman—some signal of alliance. "What's wrong with you? Hung up on that light skinned girl?"

"Hey, relax, okay? It was just some stupid kids."

"Not you, too, homeboy? Going soft on me?"

That's when Zak emerged from the school, and when he saw Herman and Tyrone and Yvonne he wanted to turn around and take another exit, but it was too late—they had already seen him.

"Hey, Herman," he said as he walked past, trying to act casual.

"Hey, Hayseed," Herman said. "What's up?"

"Not much, another day at school."

"It wasn't you who wrote that shit on the bathroom wall, was it?" Tyrone said.

"No, I don't do graffiti, or go into girls' bathrooms for that matter." Zak said. "We have better things to do in Vermont, like tipping cows." He had hoped for a laugh, but Herman was looking past him, over his shoulder, and then said, "Hi, beautiful." He turned in time to see Ivy walk up behind him.

"Hi," she said. "My name's Ivy, by the way, not beautiful. Hi, Zak."

"Hi Ivy."

"What's up?" Herman said, and Zak, kind of sensing this meeting had been planned, decided to continue on his journey. "See you later. I have to go study," he lied, and then felt foolish, and when he was halfway through the park, he glanced back at them, still talking.

"*Hi beautiful*," he muttered to himself. Where do people come up with this shit? He had a sudden yearning for one of Nick's cigarettes, and felt tired and frayed, like someone had peeled off one of his layers of skin, leaving only six. He was starting to feel like a sixteen year old loser, walking home through the cold gray damp of a dreary winter afternoon. Or was it still fall? It was cold, a low gray sky overhead, a few snowflakes drifting down in a cold wind. And now some punks had decided to write some garbage on the bathroom wall. Poor white trash—even this probably applied to half of his friends back in Vermont—farmers kids, and carpenters, and men who worked for the town, wives who made some extra money on the side, washing clothes, or dishes in the public schools. He had never thought of his friends as particularly racist— they saved most of their jokes for the ethnic groups in town, 'Wops' for Italians, and 'Pollacks' for the Poles, and the occasional Puerto Rican joke slipping in. "Hey—how did the Puerto Ricans get to America?"

"Got me?"

"One swam, and the rest walked across on the oil slick." Peels of laughter would follow, and it all seemed harmless enough, especially as there were no Puerto Rican's at Olney High School—a couple Asian kids, and one Black kid, in Zack's freshman year. And now this—getting a crush on a pretty Black girl already being chased by Mr. Basketball. All he wanted right now was to not go home to the empty, creaking apartment, and smoke a cigarette. Maybe he would buy a pack, finally.

It always seemed colder when there was no snow on the ground, for some reason. He walked across the empty expanse of the college campus, tired looking geniuses walking and talking and blowing steam into the air. When he got to the Avenue he surprised himself by turning into the tobacco shop—a pleasant, old room filled with the wonderful scent of smoke—glass jars filled with cigars and endless assortment of pipes, and a carved, wooden Indian holding a tomahawk.

"May I help you?" asked a young man behind the counter.

"Ah, yes, a pack of Marlboros, please," he said, then added, for effect, "lights."

"For your mom, right?" the man said.

"No, actually my step dad—my parents are divorced, and he's in a wheelchair, but we can't get him to quit."

"Sounds like bull to me. Next time, send your mamma, Okay? I'm not supposed to sell to minors."

"Alright," Zack said, slipping the box into his top pocket, as he had seen people do in the movies about a thousand times before. So it was that easy to kill yourself—just do that, a thousand times, or so, for the next twenty-five years.

He walked down to the coffee shop in the square, a kind of boxy, glassed in room that was jutting out into the sidewalk. He went in, ordered a hot chocolate from the pretty Spanish girl at the counter, and sat by the window,

at a small table with an ashtray—one of the last places in town where you
could still smoke—that's why the high school kids still liked it. He took a
few sips of his hot chocolate, and then 'sparked her up', as Nick would have
said. The taste was bad, but good, and he had to try hard not to cough, just
sat there in a swirling, bluish cloud of his own making, brooding. But then,
through the window he saw Ivy crossing the street and coming towards him,
heading to the subway, alone for once, and normally he would have gotten
nervous and let her pass, but he was in a strange mood and without really
thinking about it he stubbed out his cigarette, stood up and went to the door
and called out her name. She heard him on the first try, smiled and walked
back towards him.

"What are you doing here?"

"Just sitting. You want to come in for a minute?"

"Alright," she said. "I'm freezing out here." She followed him back inside
and sat down across the small table, keeping her coat on. His cigarette was
still smoking.

"I'm impressed. Hot chocolate. Nice."

"You want one?"

"No thanks." Ivy said. "I can't stay long. You come here a lot?"

"No, first time. I didn't feel like going home, or walking around with Nick,
for that matter."

"I thought he was your best friend."

"*Only* friend—there's a slight difference."

"Poor boy," Ivy said, her face breaking out into a sly smile. "You just
moved here, right?"

"Yeah, in September, from beautiful Vermont. Where's Herman?" he asked,
wanting to steer away from Vermont, and his recent family history.

"I don't know—it's not my week to baby sit."

Zak laughed. "Good one. But I thought you two were close friends."

"Friends—not close. Though he might like to think so."

"I see," Zak said, and decided not to press his luck.

"What's up with all the crap going on at school?"

"What stuff?" Ivy said. "It's freezing in here." She wrapped her arms around
herself.

"The graffiti artists."

"Oh, that." Ivy shrugged. "It happens every year—someone does something
stupid, calls someone a name, a fight breaks out, everyone talks about it for a
couple of weeks and then it goes away. The kids will get suspended for a week,
and then come back, and nothing will have changed. It's an annual event,
sponsored by the racial awareness committee. In a few weeks we'll all be
hugging in the halls again—the great happy melting pot of America."

"I can't wait," Zak said.

"I wouldn't worry about it—there's lots of stupid kids around who want attention. It will pass."

"That's good to know."

"Anyway, I better go," Ivy said, standing up. "Homework."

She was taller than he thought. "Thanks for the hot chocolate." She looked down at him as she buttoned her coat against the cold.

"You said you didn't want one." Zack protested.

She was smiling. "Joke. I'm just playing. Don't be so gullible. Next time, maybe. And by the way, smoking's not cool—in case you haven't heard." She patted the place on her where Zak's cigarettes were, in his upper left pocket, and winked.

"Thanks for the tip." Zack said, "I thought it would make me more popular, that's all."

"Yeah, right," Ivy said. "See you tomorrow." She smiled and turned and pushed out the door, and Zack watched her through the window as she walked away, just another pretty girl in the city.

"Ouch," he said softly, then sat for a moment, adjusting to her absence. "Next time," she had said.

He left a couple of dollars on the table and then went out again into the cold, the damp gray air closing in, sparking up a cigarette for company, taking up the sidewalk with his long, country-ish strides.

Up South

Ivy did an extra lap around the block, looking though the store-front windows before she went down into the subway half tempted to go back for a hot chocolate. Why had she run off? In truth, she really would have liked to have stayed there and talked to him, had a hot chocolate, to warm her up from this fucking weather. Still wet behind the ears, her Grandmother would have said of Zak, not that Ivy was so sophisticated herself, but she had grown up in the city, at least, and knew a little bit of what was going on.

Down in the subway the guitar player was not there—just the same, stale wind sweeping up the tunnel, pressed forward by the arriving train. It was half empty, and a man halfway down the car changed his seat so he could sit, she knew, across from Ivy, gawking, and running his eyes up and down her body, her legs, kind of half smiling to himself the whole time. He got off at the stop before hers, winking at her through the dirty glass, and Ivy had to hold herself back from giving him the finger. It had started when she was only thirteen, twelve even—the strange, unwanted stares of men she did not know. Yet, she had to admit to herself that she took a secret pride in the fact that men seemed to find her attractive, beautiful; it all depended in the way they looked at her. Maybe they were dogs, as Yvonne liked to say. But her father wasn't like that, though maybe her Uncle Charlie from North Carolina would qualify, as he was said to have about ten kids scattered around the county, most of them born after he got married.

By the time she got home, her mother had already set the table for dinner and her father was there, sitting in his chair with his uniform on, reading the paper. "How's school, baby?" he said.

"Alright, Dad, but I'm not really a baby, you know."

He peered over the top of the paper at her, and said, "Oh, you're all grown up, then? Look out!" Then he laughed, and Ivy laughed too. "You know you're in trouble," her father went on, "when you can't even call your own daughter 'baby.' You know something's going on—maybe someone else is calling her baby, now?"

"No one's calling me *baby*, Daddy," she said, "It's too lame, for one thing. Maybe in the seventies it was cool, but not in 1993." She walked over and he pulled her to him and laughed, and she inhaled the familiar fragrance of her father, tobacco and sweat and cologne, the starch of his uniform. "Yup," he repeated softly, still holding her to him. "Getting too old to be called baby . . . that's kind of sad." He relaxed his hold on her, drifting back to his paper. Ivy got up and walked into the kitchen, where her mother was cooking over the stove.

"Hi honey," she said. "How was school?"

"Alright, except for some racist graffiti artists on the loose in the girls' room."

"Did they find out who?"

"Yeah, two pitiful white guys, and one Spanish boy. They're suspended. They'll probably get expelled."

"I would hope so," her mother said quietly. "I thought that non-sense was over with."

"Over with?" Her father said. "Maybe in the next millennium—it's coming, you know, and only the second time since Christ. Seven years. Maybe we'll all be swallowed up and roast for all eternity in the raging fires of hell," he laughed. "That would be interesting—a little hell and damnation." And then he added, "In the army, we'd have them locked up for a month or two, and then they'd get their asses kicked out."

"Please don't talk like that, Calvin," Ivy's mother said.

"Why not—White folks do all the time," he said, and chuckled. "They can't even keep it at home—they have to write it all over the bathroom walls."

"In any case," Ivy added, "one of their asses wasn't exactly white."

Both her parents looked at her, but it was her mother who spoke. "Ivy, please don't talk like that."

"I was just quoting my good father."

"And don't be fresh, either. Just because he has a foul mouth, doesn't mean you have to, either."

"Because he's a man, you mean, and men talk like that, so it's OK?"

"Ivy, please." she said.

"In any case, they're just dumb kids."

"Yes, and in another year," her father said, "they'll be dumb adults, pulling on a white sheet every other Saturday night after the bowling league." He chuckled.

Her mother looked at him and rolled her eyes.

"Not up here, husband, please."

"No?" he said, chuckling. "Keep reading the paper—you'll see. You remember what we used to call it back home, don't you? 'Up south.' It's not so different."

"Well," her mother said, "It's unfortunate that, in this day in age, we still have these problems."

"Always have, always will. Having slick Willie in the White House won't change anything. They say he's the first black President, but heck, just liking Black women, having a single parent, and growing up in a trailer don't make you Black. Just ask Cap'n Charlie, as we used to call him."

"Don't you have to get to work very soon, my dear husband?"

"Yes," he said, folding the paper and getting up from the table, "don't want to keep Uncle Tom—I mean Uncle Sam—waiting."

"Calvin, please." his wife said. "Ivy, can you call Junior?"

Ivy walked down the hall to her brother's room where he had plugged himself into a computer game. He was a small, shy boy with glasses who had not yet acquired either Ivy's good looks, nor his father's blustery self-confidence. But he was smart, and preferred computers to people—top of his class at Hopewell Junior High. He and Ivy got along, but mostly kept to themselves: "I have two only children," her mother liked to say. His father worried the boy wasn't tough enough to stand up to the kids who had already started to prey on him, hassling him when he got out of school. "We got to toughen him up," he was fond of saying, "and find him a spot, somewhere beside the chess team."

"For what?" he mother would answer. "He's not going to have to fight; he's smart."

"And I'm not?" her husband said. "You still have to fight sometimes."

"Yeah, maybe with your brain, not just your fists."

"Now what is that supposed to mean?"

"Can we eat, please?" Ivy said, and then asked, "Mom, can I go the dance Friday night?"

"What dance?" her father said. "And, with who? Pass the potatoes please."

"With *whom*, you mean. Yvonne, and a couple friends of hers—Herman and Tyrone."

"And who are Herman and Tyrone, pray tell?" asked her mother.

"A couple guys in my class—they're alright."

"Alright? I think we can do better than 'alright'" her father said. Ivy rolled her eyes. "I want to see these two characters before you go anywhere. And Yvonne, too, for that matter. She's not exactly an angel, as I remember."

"Yeah, her and all the other girls at school." Ivy said, and her father paused in his eating, and looked up at her. "Don't worry, Dad. I'm not out of the house long enough to drink a milkshake—I'm not even allowed to go to the school dance, even though my grades are good, and behind my back everyone calls me Miss Goody Two Shoes, because I still dress like it's a Catholic School. They think I'm acting White." Her mother looked at Ivy, and her brother, and then gently lay her fork down on her plate as if, otherwise, she would be tempted to throw it across the room.

"No, I don't know where these kids get the idea that trying to do well in school, get good grades, and get into a good college and not have three babies by the time you're seventeen is trying to 'act white'. When my parents were growing up, it was just trying to make something of yourself—getting out of the cotton field or the kitchen, scrubbing someone else's floors, and drawers, saying Yes, mam, a hundred times a day." Her voice was getting stronger, and then she paused, pulling herself back. "For the life of me, I don't know how trying to do well in school, for yourself and your family, got to be a bad thing."

"We can see that," her husband said, "It's good to see a little fire and brimstone now and then. As for acting White, I have nothing against it, as long as it doesn't turn into marrying White. I don't care what they say—there's plenty of good Black men around, right son?" he asked, thumping Junior on the shoulder.

"If you say so, dad."

"Well, I do, and eat some potatoes. If you're going to be in the Army man, like my boy Colin Powell, you better put some meat on those bones—you can't get through life with brains alone."

"And why is that?" Ivy asked, still mulling over his commentary.

"Because sometimes," her father said, taking the mock stance of a boxer, "you got to stand up and take some hits, and then give some back, only harder!!"

"Yeah," Ivy said "and that's why kids my age are getting shot up every day."

"Because they're cowards," her father countered, "No one ever taught them how to fight like a real man, with your fists—no guns or knives or sticks: your two hands—and see how they feel afterwards, after they've punched someone's head a few times, and had their's knocked around too. You might think twice the next time."

"Depends on the head, I guess," Ivy said, glancing at him. "Some are thicker than others, I hear."

He glanced over at her. "Smart mouth, this girl. I wonder where she got that from?"

"Gee, let's see," her mother said, scratching her head. "I can't imagine."

"And I don't think anyone," Ivy added, "should tell anyone else who to date—if you love the person, that should be enough."

"Who said anything about dating—I said marry. Hell, I dated a few light-skinned women myself," he said, with a little wink, "*before* I had the good fortune to find your mother, that is."

"Light, not white," His mother said. "Anyway, this isn't exactly dinner table conversation."

"It won't kill us." Ivy said.

"No, but it will ruin our dinner."

"A dance . . ." her father said, "As far as I'm concerned, the young lady can go to the dance, as long as she's home by midnight, as least—one a.m. on the outside. You know your mother can't sleep until you get home." He put down his napkin and stood up.

"Besides," he added, grinning slyly, "I never met any White boys named Herman and Tyrone, I can bet you on that." Then he laughed, a great, deep rumble of mirth rising up from somewhere inside him, filling the room. Even his wife and Ivy and Junior had to smile. He was still talking as he went out the door. "No sir—Herman and Tyrone, those are my boys. As long as they come around here first and tell me they're going to do right, and then they'll see what they're in for, in case they get any ideas."

"Goodbye Calvin," Ivy's mother said. "Don't let the door hit you on the way out."

"Tough women," he said to himself, and then he was gone, the sound of his own footsteps chasing him out the door.

"What light-skinned women?" Ivy asked her over the dishes, after Junior had gone back to his computer games.

"Your father likes to boast, if he's in the mood. In any case, we didn't meet until he was twenty-six, I was nineteen, so I guess he had a couple of women before that. But I guess he fell in love pretty fast, and that was the end of that. Two months later, we were married, off in the train to our honeymoon in Charleston."

"And he was the only man you were ever with?" Ivy asked. Ivy's mother stopped in mid-dish and looked over at her.

"What do you mean *with*, young lady?"

"Oh, Mom," Ivy said, "You know what I mean."

"No I don't, exactly. He was my first boyfriend, if that's what you're asking. And that's all I care to discuss."

"Good enough, Mom. I don't want to pry." That's when her mother gave up her dish towel and sat down at the kitchen table, looked up at her with her sad and beautiful brown eyes, but it was Ivy who spoke first. "Yes, mom, I'm still a virgin, if that's what you're about to ask. How could I not be—I never go anywhere, and I have no male friends."

"It doesn't take long."

"Really? I didn't know that! I thought you had to have sex three or four times to get pregnant. Sorry, mom—but I do know how babies are made. You told me when I was thirteen, remember? Plus, they've been reminding us every year since we were ten or so, in case we forgot over the summer. KYB: know your body."

"I know, Ivy . . . it just seems like girls your age are under a lot of pressure, and everyone has to grow up so fast, and you have such a future in front of you."

"I know all that Mom, and I'm not about to mess it up, alright? You don't get pregnant by dancing, last I heard."

"The way some of these people dance on TV, it's a wonder they don't!" she laughed.

"You go to your dance, and have fun. It's just that, your father and I came up in a different place, and a different time. I barely finished high school, never mind college. Back then even most White women didn't go to college, never mind a poor Black girl from South Carolina. And your father's a smart, ambitious man, but if it wasn't for the Army, we might be back home working for the PO, or something. He may seem a little strict, sometimes, but he's just looking out for you." Then she paused, and looked up at her. "You're a smart and beautiful young woman," she said, "and that's something to hold onto."

"I'm glad someone finally used the word 'woman'." Ivy said. "The way people have been talking, you'd think I was ten years old."

"Anyone with eyes can see that you're a woman." her mother said, "That's part of the problem for girls—their bodies grow up before they do. And if you're pretty, it's even worse—the women are jealous, and the men are after you all the time . . . Now that I think of it, your grandparents weren't too happy when I brought your father home, either."

"Why?"

"Well, even though we had no money, we were always pretty high on ourselves, and some people thought marrying your father would be a step in the wrong direction—downwards, that is."

"Because he was too dark?"

"That was part of it, plus, his daddy was a dirt farmer, and I guess my parents thought they were a little better than that." When her mother talked about growing up, she noticed, her voice returned to the soft, rolling cadences of the south.

"So what happened?"

"Well, I was pretty headstrong, and they could see I had made up my mind, and that if they didn't like it, we'd head off and do it—get married, that is—anyway. So they decided to go along with it, and that's the way it happened. Some of my aunts were a little dicty at the wedding, but they got used to it pretty fast—they had no choice. People get over it. Sometimes in life, you have to make up your own mind about things—as long as you're old enough, that is."

"O.K., Mom. I get the idea—I'm lucky to have parents who care about me, and all that, right?"

"Yes. And now, you better go answer your phone. It's rung about ten times since we've been sitting here."

"That's what machines are for," Ivy said, gave her a hug and then went down the hall to her room.

Losers

Outside, it was colder than Zak had thought, and a couple stars flickered down on them from a frozen sky—two high school losers striking out in search of adventure.

"Where to, homey?" Nick said, lighting up a cigarette, hunching himself against the cold. He was wearing a thin, tired, suede jacket that looked like it had seen action in the Wild West.

"Let's go check out the dance. It's too cold for the pit."

"Alright. Maybe some girls will take pity on us and ask us to dance."

"Don't make me nervous," Zak said. "And hand over a cigarette."

"Face it—you're hooked," Nick grinned.

Outside the school kids were hanging out in the darkness, padding their feet against the cold, and from inside came the muffled thump of music.

"How is it in there?" Nick asked them.

"Dead."

"Great. It was a nice walk, anyway."

"I'm going in," Zak said.

"Go for it." Nick said. "I'm here."

At the door sat Mr. Nicolosi and Ms. Rigaud, another math teacher. "Good evening, Zak." he said, and stamped his hand with a weak blue tattoo that said "UNITY".

There was something nice about walking around an empty school at night, along the quiet, corridors, towards the thumping of music that flooded out of the gym. Inside, it was dark, and a few lights swirled across the floor, and a few kids sat against the walls, watching a single couple dance.

"Hi, Zak." someone said, and from the shadows emerged Heather, she of the golden, beaded dreadlocks. She was wearing a halter top that left her pale belly bare, and exposed the golden loop of a belly button ring. "Hi, Heather," Zak said, looking down at her stomach. "Nice, ah, jewelry . . ."

"Thanks."

"It doesn't hurt?"

"Does it look like it hurts?"

"Ah . . . well, yes."

"Well, it doesn't, so don't fret. You came alone?"

"No, my date is outside—Nick, the bearded wonder, but he's out getting high."

"Cool." Heather said. "Let's join him."

"No thanks. This is a 'drug free zone', remember?"

"Oh yeah."

As they stood and talked in the dim light of the gym, his eyes kept wandering along the curves of her body to the smooth, pale skin of her belly, which seemed slightly odd, somehow—fuller, slightly rounder, than it should have been. She had a pretty face, light freckles on her high cheekbones, pale eyebrows. She was wearing no bra, her breasts held loosely in a half cashmere sweater, like some type of wonderful, unobtainable fruit—'sweater puppies', as some of the kids back in Vermont used to say.

"What are you smiling about?" Heather asked.

"Nothing much." Zak said, blushing. "Just an old, dumb joke, I remember."

"It must be a good one—you're blushing."

Kids were drifting into the gym—Spanish girls in long, shiny dresses, boys in fancy satin suits, others in their baggy pants and gym suits.

"I didn't know we were supposed to dress up." he said.

"We're not," Heather said. "You look fine—for a country boy. Why do they call you that, anyway?"

"Because I'm from Vermont, I guess. They can't think of anything better. Where's *your* boyfriend, anyway?" he asked her.

"I don't have one—just friends. I'm too young to be committed."

"Yeah, me too." Zak said. "That's what I always tell them when they want to get serious."

Just then an entourage walked by in a cloud of perfume and cologne, and as they drifted away Zak could see who it was—Herman and Tyrone, then Yvonne's hour glass body pulled into a tight red dress, and beside her was Ivy, in a dress the same shade of brown as her skin so that, for an instant, it looked like she might be naked.

"Geesh." he said to himself.

"What?" Heather asked, following them with her eyes.

"Nothing."

"Yeah, right." Heather said. "I know what you're looking at. You like that girl, don't you?"

"Who?"

"You know who—not booty queen, the other one, her friend."

"Ivy? We're in homeroom together. Yeah, it's true: sometimes I say 'Good morning.'"

"I saw you with her in the pit one day."

"You see everything, don't you? That was the only time I've ever talked to her, actually, outside of class, almost."

"Whatever—you can talk to whoever you want around here," she said and winked. "I'll catch you later." There were two tears in her jeans, in the middle of her ass, and she walked they opened and closed, like winking eyes: she was wearing turquoise underwear. It was darker, now, and louder, and there were more aimless teenagers drifting around the floor in little packs, waiting for something to happen. A few kids were dancing.

They were trying hard to please everyone with the music, and every few songs it would change—some for the Spanish kids, some for the Black kids, some for the Haitians and West Indians, hip hop, rap. Heather was having no problems, though, and whenever new music came on, there she would be on the dance floor, arms spread wide, drifting around like a great, pale bird. Sometimes she danced alone, other times she would be joined by some hopeful boy, but when they figured out she wasn't really dancing with them, just near them, they drifted away. Between songs, she saw Zak standing alone and grabbed one of his hands.

"I forget how." he protested.

"Like it's so hard." She took his hand and pulled him out onto the floor, and he had no choice but to move. Luckily, it was dark, and he had Heather's body to contemplate, and her pretty, serene face, and then she leaned toward him, smiling, and said, "See—it's simple." Then she whirled around, and bumped into someone who then turned and looked at her—it was Ivy.

"Sorry." Heather shouted, over the music, and Ivy raised her hand to say O.K., and Ivy glanced over at Zak and waved. She was dancing not with Herman, but with Tyrone, and Herman seemed to be dancing with Yvonne, one of his hands resting on the deep shelf of her waist. She had done something with her hair, so that it hung in loose, curls around her face, and her lips were painted a bright red. But he was mostly aware of Ivy near him, and without Heather noticing him he watched her as she danced, watched as Tyrone tried to get closer to her, to touch her, but then she would drift away, as if she did not notice. She looked taller in a dress, her body swaying loosely in the thin cloth.

Then a slow song came on, and Zak was about to retreat to the edges of the dance floor when Heather took him by the hand and pulled him toward him, and the next thing he knew he was holding her body lightly in his arms, his hands on the small of her back, hers draped over his shoulders, her naked stomach pressed against his.

"It's only a dance." she said to him, "relax."

"I am—can't you tell?" He tried to follow the rhythms of her body, the way her legs scissored against his, the fragrance of her locks as they swayed before him. His hands drifted down to where her bare back began to swell into her hips in the mysterious way of womens' bodies. He could feel the vague softness of her breasts pressing against him, and he could see Ivy and Yvonne, back with their respective dates, held close and barely moving except for the slow, circular motion of their hips, which he tried not to think about—looked off into the room, and tried to solve algebra problems in his head. And then the song was winding down, and he was letting his hand drift around her back, and Zak was hoping the song would not end soon, wished Heather would take him with her when she left, take him to some dim lit place and make love to him, like Jill Stevens had once, sort of, the night he almost lost his virginity, at her parent's ski house in the Northeast Kingdom. But it had only happened once, and just when Zak thought he had a girlfriend at last, she had returned to her regular boyfriend, geeky Beaver Perkins, a year older and back from his fancy college for the summer.

Then the song was over, his hand slid down her back and off her ass like a ski jump (no underwear) and then she was gone, drifting away across the room. To his irritation, Nick Price appeared from the shadows, a bearded phantom, and said "Way to go, Zakster. I had no idea. Heather Macdonald—she's one of the hottest girls in the school."

"Gee, that's good to know." Zak said. "I'll put it in my college applications—'danced with Heather McDonald, once'."

The music had stopped and a pleasant silence was settling over the room. Zak watched as Tyrone and Herman left and Herman, seeing him there, raised his fist and said, "Yo, Hayseed, how's it going?"

"Alright, Herman. And you?" Zak had started to drop syllables, he noticed, when talking to Herman.

"Chillin, man." Herman said, and Tyrone just kind of looked at Nick and Zak with a kind of withering amusement. Ivy and Yvonne set off on a slow, meandering tour of the room—two beauties of Central High, walking with sauntering rhythm of teenaged girls who know that pairs of eyes—mens' and womens' both—are following them as they walked.

The president of the class, Roman Riverez, a handsome "A" student wearing something like a tuxedo, only shinier, was giving a speech of some sort, on the theme of unity—how we all have to stick together, and we can't let some simple minded bigots divide us, and how when he looked around at the room, he saw lots of little groups, each looking at the others, and he wanted to see some people mixing it up, for a change. Roman had already mixed it up himself, somewhat, as he was dating Claudine Henry, considered one of the hottest Black girls. The Dominican girls didn't like it much, called him a sellout, and the Black guys didn't like it much, called *her* a 'sellout' behind her back, but what could they say—he was smart, handsome, the president of the class. And Claudine Henry was smart and beautiful, the daughter of a doctor, going to Yale like he had. He could get any girl he wanted, or so they said.

"No thanks." Zak heard Yvonne say behind him, rather loudly. "Unless Roman wants to dump Claudine, maybe then I'd think about. He's so fine—but I don't date Spanish dudes." Zak turned in time to see her suck her teeth, and then walk away, swinging for emphasis. Ivy Whitman looked back at Zak, smiled, and said, "She really didn't mean that."

"No?"

"Not really." She had turned to follow Yvonne, but then stepped back toward Zak. "She says a lot of things. I never really worried too much about what comes out of her mouth." Over her shoulder, Zak saw Herman and Tyrone heading out the door. "There goes your date." he said, nodding towards them.

"*Friend*—barely." Ivy said.

"You better let *him* know that."

"I have, plenty of times. Anyway, where's your *friend*? I didn't know you two were so close."

Girls always liked you better, Zak had noticed, when they saw you talking to other girls, like it gave you some kind of stamp of approval—USAD approved. "We're not—she just took pity on me and asked me to dance."

"I could see that," Ivy said. "A slow dance, no less. You should consider yourself honored—she usually only goes with rastas."

"I'll grow locks."

Ivy laughed, surprising him, her face tipped back toward the ceiling, showing the beautiful shape of her collar bone, like wings. "You should," she said. "That would be cute."

"You, too."

Ivy rolled her eyes. "Yeah, right. My parents would love that—they can barely let me out to a chaperoned, school dance—never mind growing locks."

"Braids, then." Zak was trying to show his newly acquired knowledge of Black girls' hair styles.

"If I ever cut my hair short my father would throw a fit, so here I am—Miss Brown Barbie doll of Carver High." She stroked her hair. Zak decided not to reveal his ignorance by asking what was involved in getting your hair straightened—"fried", as Ms. Newman said.

"Your hair looks fine."

"Sure, but I have to have it relaxed every three weeks—fifty bucks a time. It's a waste of money."

The band was reassembling up on the stage, loudly tuning their guitars, and Ivy glanced back over her shoulder in search of her entourage but they were nowhere in sight. Even Yvonne had not yet returned.

"Maybe they're out smoking herb with Nick," Zak said.

"They better not be, or I'm taking a cab home."

"Now remember," Ramon was saying from the stage, "Let's have everyone dance, alright—and I mean everyone!"

"We are the world." Ivy said dubiously, rolling her eyes.

Zak was starting to get nervous about whether he was supposed to ask her to dance, and she kept glancing over her shoulder to see if her friends were coming back, and then the music started, and the lights got dim again, and even though it was old time music kids drifted out onto the floor. Before he could say anything, Ivy said "I like this song. Come on."

Zak was shy, but no fool, and they moved out into the floor, and he tried not to think too much about his body, what it was or wasn't doing. And as they danced, she mouthed the words to the song, and he watched her face in the shifting colors, watched the slight concavity in her dress where her belly button was, her body moving in a languorous motion, like a reed underwater he had seen in some lame under the sea show on public television. He tried not to stare but his eyes kept returning to her, and when the song melted into another one they kept dancing. He wanted to reach out to the curve of her waist and pull her toward him, but didn't dare, yet. Out of the corner of his eye he caught a glimpse of red, Yvonne, and Herman standing by the edge of the dance floor, and Zak leaned over and said, "You'd better go."

"The song's not over yet."

"Yeah, but . . ."

"Relax—he doesn't own me. Besides, where have *they* been?"

But when the song did end, and Zak said "Thanks, talk to you later," and Ivy smiled and went over to talk to Herman.

"Don't stop on my account." Herman said.

"You're the one who disappeared."

"Just went out for a smoke."

"Of what?" Ivy asked, and she could tell by the way Herman sort of half smiled, by the way his eyes took on a slightly glazed look, and red, that it wasn't tobacco.

"I don't like that." Ivy said, and looked out onto the dance floor where a slow dance was starting up.

"Come on." Herman said, and wrapped his hands around her waist, and this was the last that Zak saw of them, locked in a kind of bear hug, Ivy looking away across the room, over his shoulder, her lithe body pressed tightly against his. "Let's get out of here." he said to Nick, who was looking rather glazed and red eyed himself. "This is painful to watch."

"You sure you want to go?" Nick asked. "Looks like you're on a roll. You might get lucky."

"Yeah, right," Zak said. "I think my luck is over for the night."

"Cool." Nick said. On their way out the door into the frigid air, someone said, "Bye Zak," and he glanced around at Heather, who was standing close to some smooth talking hippie who was trying to grow some flat, stringy locks. "Leaving so soon?"

"Yeah", Zak said. "I have a curfew. I'll turn into a pumpkin if I don't get home soon. See you later, Heather."

"Bye, Zak. See you later, Nick."

"Bye Heather." Nick said. "Peace." And then, when they were out of earshot, and he was sparking up a cigarette, he added. "Wow, Zak-meister. I better hang with you more often."

"Hey, you're cool, Nick. What can I say?" And then they bumped fists, in the style of true Rasta men everywhere.

Sleep

When Ivy came in that night, just after one, she found her father sitting in the armchair, in the dim light, his mouth slightly ajar, as if he were waiting for a fly to pass by to catch and eat. But as she stood looking at him, wondering if he was breathing, he said, "Good evening, angel. Or should I say "Good morning?" He glanced at the watch he had left by the table. "Twelve thirty three—not bad. Where's your escort? I thought he was supposed to come in and pay his respects."

"At one in the morning?" Ivy said, but in truth the night had ended badly, and she didn't think it was the best idea to have Herman come up with his eyes blood shot, besides having an attitude about Ivy not wanting to go to an after party. Then he had walked her to the door, and clumsily tried to kiss her there, but Ivy had turned her head away, offering her cheek. She was still upset that they had all gone out to smoke herb, and didn't like the comments Yvonne had made about her dancing with that "white boy."

"Did you have fun?" Her father said to her now as she came into the room, pulling himself up out of the chair where he had been quietly sleeping.

"A little."

"Give me a hug, then, before I sleep." he said, and Ivy felt herself surrounded by his arms, pressed against the shape of his body, enveloped by the fragrance that hovered around him, that reminded her of summer down south, the scent that blew off the sun baked land and rattled the leaves of the trees and came in through the billowing curtains of her grandmother's house, reminding her of her childhood

He kissed her on the forehead and was moving through the dim light toward the bedroom, looking tired. Then he paused and looked back at her. "Thanks for coming home on time—you saved me a night in the un-easy chair—never could sleep until you got home."

"No problem, Dad. I need to sleep, too. See you in the morning."

"Goodnight, Ivy. Sleep well."

"You too, daddy."

There were messages on the machine, too—five of them, but she wasn't going to listen. She turned off the ringer, and put the phone under a pile of Teddy bears so she wouldn't hear it when they called to tell them how much fun they were having without her. After her shower she got in a night gown and lay in the soft light of the room, looking up at the ceiling, thinking about the evening, wondering why she couldn't get along better with Herman. She had liked dancing with him, actually, liked the way he felt with his arms wrapped around her, the way his body pressed against her, the strange, gathering urgency of something below his waist, a certain hardness, the way his hands kept sliding down the curve of her back almost to her ass; she would have let him kiss her at the door to her house but by that time he had already caught an attitude about her not going to the after party, and when the moment had come she had turned her cheek, and Herman had said, "Ah, man . . . not this again," and before she had a chance to change her mind he had turned quickly, gone down to the car and sped off. And now they were all driving around to parties, getting drunk and high, talking trash about her. Let them. She lay on her back and let her hands drift restlessly along the smooth skin of her body, her belly, down to her swelling hips and then down along her strong, firm thighs, upwards to the place where all the lines of her body converged, a confluence of all of a woman's vulnerability and power, a place her grandmother once called her 'womanhood'—a strangely powerful word that evoked all sorts of mysteries she was not ready for. Then her hands moved back up her hips, her belly, up her ribs, to her breasts that wanted to be touched, held by someone *else's* hands, kissed by someone's lips, as described in some of those books that Yvonne had showed her. Was this what boys wanted? Her whole body seemed to grow warmer, and suddenly she wished she had let Herman kiss her, and thought about that boy down south, and the way his lips had pressed against hers, and she thought, too, of Zak, who kept re-appearing in her life, and the way she had an impulse to tease him, and whenever she tried he always surprised her, like he knew what she was thinking. And although dancing didn't seem to be something they did a whole lot of back in Vermont, he had done alright, and she would have liked to continue, but he got scared off by Herman; as they walked off the floor he had touched her, a light, but certain touch somewhere in the vicinity of her waist or lower, and this too had surprised her: maybe he was not as shy, as innocent as he sometimes seemed—who knows what they did up there in the woods and fields, out in the country? What did she know about White boys? Not very much—the usual stereotypes— can't jump, can't dance, can't "do it", as Yvonne liked to say, had small you-know-whats. Yvonne and her friends liked to sit on a bench outside the school watching the boys walk by, assessing "what they got" by the bulges in their pants, or lack thereof, a pastime Ivy did not particularly find amusing, and kind of cruel, like boys sitting around rating womens' asses.

She'd rather picture his face, his eyes (blue, or gray—she could never decide) the way he looked over her shoulder in homeroom pretending he wasn't trying to talk to her, but she knew everything about him was quietly focused on her, leaning towards her, but he was too shy to speak, or at least pretended he was—she wasn't sure which. "May I help you?" she wanted to say. "You are staring." She would have to find a way to talk to him, let him know it was cool, she wasn't going to bite.

Then she had grown tired of thinking, and her hands stopped their restless migrations over her body and settled, finally, in the soft, warm valley of her belly, her breathing rose and fell in waves, and she fell into a deep and sudden sleep, pleasantly devoid of dreams.

Winter

Suddenly the quarter was over and in a week it would be Christmas. Then it snowed, and rained, and everything froze, and the weather turned cold and depressing and gray. Gaudy Christmas lights were hung above the dreary avenue and swung in the wind. Back in Vermont for a week Zak hung around with his old friends, and stayed with his father, but his mother never came there, to their old house, but stayed with friends on the other side of town. Now and then a woman would call the house asking for "Mr. Walker, please"; and then one day, while he was out Christmas shopping with his father at the mall they had run into a woman with blond hair, a few years younger than his mother, though slightly less pretty, who had been introduced to him as "Margaret." And there was something strange in the awkward silence that followed, and they looked at each other, and then at Zak, and then his father said feebly, "Well, see you later." and the woman looked surprised, said 'goodbye', and walked quickly away.

Later in the car, Zak surprised even himself by blurting out, "So that's your new girlfriend?" and his father, as if expecting the question, said, "We're friends," and then launched into an unsolicited speech about himself and Zak's mother, and how things hadn't always been easy between them, and how, now that Zak was older, and it seemed like a good time to try something new, and . . .

"So why didn't we stay here with you?" Zak said, his voice quavering. "Why did we have to get shipped off to that idiot city? Why couldn't we stay here and finish school while you and Mom split up?"

His father was silent for a minute, as if he had not really thought of this possibility, and then said, not very loudly, "It's what your mother wanted. It seemed like the best idea at the time. She wanted you with her."

And you got to stay here with your girlfriend? Zak wanted to say, but didn't.

"I know it hasn't been easy on anyone, these changes." his father said, pulling into the driveway of the house where they all once lived as a perfect, "nuclear" family, whatever that meant—maybe that it could explode at any minute.

"But I think for now," his father continued, "it's best for everyone."

"It's fine." Zak said, getting out of the car, trying not to slam the door. He had a strong desire to walk the five miles to the bus stop, and take it back to the city, but instead he called one of his friends and the next night he found himself sitting in the back seat of Randy Broekel's mother's car with Jill Meyers, whom he had known since childhood. Randy drove, and beside him sat Maureen Gianakopolous, a quiet, pretty girl from one of the town's few Greek families, and they drove aimlessly through the countryside, past old bars and the cold black shapes of mountains, past snow covered fields bathed in moonlight. The radio was playing, and they drank beer, and at one point he found that his knee was bumping up against hers, and then his hand somehow intertwined itself with hers, and they drove around some more, and then they parked on a deserted road next to an open field. It had snowed a couple inches the night before, and a half moon had just cleared the tops of the trees and flooded everything in a soft, pale light. In the front seat, Randy and Maureen started making out, and it didn't seem quite right to just sit there and watch, and so Zak held her hand, and looked out the window, and then said, as a kind of lame joke, "Gee, it's hot in here. Maybe we should get some fresh air."

"Why?" she said, but came out anyway, and they stood for a minute looking out across the field, listening to the quiet, the sound of trees cracking in the cold, a distant dog barking, and then, without an invitation, he was holding her, pressed between the cold car and her warm, soft body, and her warm, wet lips were pressed against his, and his hands reached up under her coat and surrounded the small of her back, her body pressing itself against his. Her long hair kept falling between them, and he held it back from her face with his hand, and they kissed for so long he had to pause to catch his breath, now and then, and then she took one of his hands and led it around to the soft, sweatered front of her and Zak could hardly believe what was happening when Randy Broekel, who was a bit of a fool, honked the horn, and scared the shit out of them.

"Come on, nature boy," Randy said. "We have to take Maureen home before her old man comes looking for us with his shotgun."

"Good idea." Zak said, and on the way he held Jill's cool hand between his. But his house was on the way, and he got out first, leaning over to kiss her before he climbed out. "Call me," she said, more of an invitation than a command, and he watched as the car pulled away over the crunching snow.

On Christmas day, his mother came over, and his father's parents, and a great aunt from over in Olney and, amidst the food and the presents and the lights of the Christmas tree and the food and the little glasses of sherry that started to appear, and disappear, it almost seemed like nothing had changed. His mother was jolly, as was his father, and at one point Zak's great-aunt whispered to him, "What's wrong with those two—look how happy they seem together!"

"Don't ask me," Zak said, and she answered, with a shake of her head, "I wish they'd just grow up, and then she laughed, "But you hang in there, kiddo. You're doing great." He had always liked Aunt Agnes.

That night was the annual Christmas party at big Jim Halloway's house, a large stone structure on the far side of town. All his friends from the old days were there, and there was a soft, yellow glow in the room, and a great brass tub filled with ice and beer, and big Jim smoking one of his large cigars and wearing a kilt, like he always did on Christmas Eve. In another room the younger teenagers hung out, playing pool and eating slices of an enormous, smoked ham. Zak's mother was there, but his father had chosen not to come, observing the unspoken moratorium of those who had left their wife or husband and taken up with someone new. And his mother seemed happy and glamorous there, with all the friends of the old crowd, and people kept coming up to her and hugging her and saying they missed her in town, and hoped all was going well for her back in the city, and when was she coming back to live in town? Zak played pool a lot that night, and kept returning to the gleaming copper bowl for cold bottles of beer, and hung around with Mathew Brown, his best friend from junior high school. There was a bunch of younger girls there, too, who weren't looking so young anymore, with their painted lips and tight fitting sweaters and hips that had suddenly appeared from nowhere.

"Jailbait," Mathew Brown said, and then the big front door opened, and it was a second before Zak recognized, through the haze of his insobriety, Randy Broekel and Maureen and, coming in behind them, in a tight fitting leather coat, Jill Meyers, she of the snow field and the soft moist lips. Through the haze and glitter of the party he watched her as she took off her coat, revealing a woman's body lightly held in a long, black dress.

"*Danger, danger, danger,*" Zak heard himself say and, like a moth to light walked over to greet them.

"Hi Zak," she said and then leaned forward to kiss him fully on the lips. "I thought you were going to call me?"

New Year

For Christmas that year, Ivy had been given by her mother a long, black dress that fit her slender, shapely body perfectly.

"My, my," her father said when she came into the room on the evening of the last day of the year.

"Does it fit?" she asked, turning around.

"A little too well for my taste, but let me hold my tongue. I'm under strict orders from your mother to let you grow up, so let me start trying now. But yes, to answer your question, it fits. Now, where do you suppose you're going, in that nice new dress?"

"To a party," Ivy's mother said, walking into the room. "We've discussed it forever, as you know, so let's leave it alone. It's New Year's Eve, if you haven't heard."

"I guess so," he said, "That's what the paper says. So who's the lucky man?"

Ivy rolled her eyes. "You know who."

"You think he'll be able to come in and talk to her folks this time?"

Ivy laughed. "Actually, Dad, I'm just going with Yvonne, to a party at her aunt's house."

"And what aunt is this—where does she live?"

"I don't know—over in Slatters, somewhere."

"The projects? Couldn't you find some better place to see in the New Year than Slatters? The only thing you hear about from there is shootings."

"Because that's all the media wants us to hear about it," Ivy said.

"Yes," her father chuckled, "and also because it's true."

The doorbell rang, and Ivy ran down the stairs and came back up.

"Here's my date, Daddy." Ivy said, and her father looked up at Yvonne, in a black fur coat, wearing beneath it a tight red dress that barely reached halfway down her thighs. "Hi, Mr. Whitman." she said, bending to give him a kiss on the cheek.

"Hi Yvonne," Ivy's mother said, coming in.

"Hi, Mrs. Whitman," Yvonne said, but they did not kiss. Beautiful women, Ivy noticed, gave each other a lot of space.

"It's hot in here," Yvonne said, and let the coat slide off her like a second skin, drooping to the chair.

"What kind of party did you say this was?" Ivy's father asked, clearing his throat.

"Your mother lets you go out in that, Yvonne?" Mrs. Whitman said.

"She has no choice. Besides, you should see what she's wearing."

"I see." Ivy's mother said, somewhat coolly.

"I'll protect her." Ivy said, handing Yvonne back her coat.

"And what time will you be home?" Her mother asked.

"Tomorrow, sometime," Ivy said, glibly.

"How about by two a.m.? And if you can't get a ride from Ms. Yvonne, here, take twenty dollars for a taxi. And you be careful—people get kind of crazy on New Year's Eve."

"Alright, Mom," Ivy said, and kissed them before she went out. "Goodnight, Mr. and Mrs. Whitman." Yvonne said, pulling the door shut behind her.

"Hmmm . . ." Mr. Whitman said, going back to his paper. "I'm glad I'm not her father—I'd never get any sleep."

"Well, she wouldn't be going out looking like that, either. Some people are growing up too, fast, that's all," she sighed. "Yvonne's alright. I don't think she gets much at home."

"The apple doesn't fall far from the tree."

It was colder outside than Ivy had thought, and the wind swept up the street, pressing before it a small whirlpool of tattered leaves and scraps of paper.

"Where's you car?" Ivy asked.

"In the shop," Yvonne said, "That's why I had to ask Tyrone for a ride, and at the last minute Herman asked if we could give him a ride, too."

"*What?*" Ivy said, and it was only then that she recognized the low, skulking shape of Tyrone's car, an old American shit-box with rust above the wheels, and in it two familiar profiles.

"Jesus, Yvonne!" Ivy said, stopping in her tracks on the sidewalk. "I thought this was supposed to be just *us*—going out to have fun on New Year's Eve."

"We can't have fun by ourselves. Besides, how are we going to get there?"

"My father could have given us a ride—he offered."

"Oh, that would have been fun," Yvonne said sarcastically. "Come on, let's go. Stop acting like a nerd—relax."

"Like a what?" Ivy said, not moving, but Yvonne had already climbed into the back seat.

"Good evening, ladies." Tyrone said, starting up the car with a growl.

"Hi, Ivy," Herman said. "How you feeling?"

"Fair." Ivy answered, and as they pulled away from the curb she glanced up at the window to see the familiar shape of her mother, looking down at them. "Oh great—now I'm going catch hell when I get home, too. I don't lie to my parents."

"Blame it on me." Yvonne said. "Did you see your father looking at me?"

"Can you shut up?" Ivy said, glaring over at her. "That's my father."

"Men are men."

Fuck You, Ivy would have liked to have said, but couldn't quite get it out. Instead she sat in silence, watching the lights of the city whiz by. Every time she thought she and Yvonne were going to have a great time, like they used to, something like this would happen—a mean word, a slight deception that Ivy had to swallow. Why did it always have to be this way?

The twenty dollars her mother had given her, in the end, turned out to be very useful. When it was about 1:13 in the morning on the first day of the year 1994 when she decided she had had enough fun, and told Yvonne she was ready to leave, and Yvonne just laughed and said, "Yeah, right. Maybe in a couple of hours." Then she went to look for Herman, to give him the bad news, and found him on the couch, pressed up against some girl he had been dancing with, pretty and light skinned beauty with freckles and a black beret, and as Ivy as she stood there, she stared up at her with the look of death. "I have to go now," she said to him, pulling the twenty dollar bill out of her purse.

"Wait—I'll walk you out." Herman said, but before he could stand up she had already grabbed her coat and walked to the door. "Don't bother. I can see you're busy. I wouldn't want you to miss your chance."

"Don't be like that, Ivy. You're not mad or anything, are you?"

"No, just tired. I already called a cab. I'll talk to you tomorrow."

"Kiss?"

Ivy offered him her cheek, and let herself be kissed.

"Happy New Year." she said, glanced once more into the room, and went outside.

It was cold and dark, and not easy to find a cab, but she finally did, and the driver was an older man with rhythms of his thick Nigerian accent. "A pretty girl should not be alone on New Year's Eve. Soon, I will get off work, and . . ." Did men just say these things out of habit, constantly testing, pushing, hoping?

"Yes—that's why I'm going home to my parents—they're about your age."

"I see," he said, and chuckled to himself. He seemed be harmless, and it was pleasant being in the back of the cab, alone, watching the lights of the city, a few drunken revelers singing on the streets. Maybe in 2000, just as she would be finishing college, the world would blow up, like some people said it would, and she would be swallowed up in the flames—the last, graduating virgin in America.

The ride used up fourteen of her twenty dollars, and she tipped him three. "Thank you, darling," he said.

Upstairs, her parents were already asleep, and there was a note from her mother. "Happy New Year, beautiful. See you in the morning. I found this letter in a pile of my bills. It's been here a few days—sorry." Ivy took the small envelope into her room, shed her clothes, drank a glass of water, and looked at the letter, postmarked somewhere, VT—Olney? She opened it quickly—it was a card, a photograph of some old men in red plaid shirts, standing next to a maple tree. Inside was a note in a strange and unfamiliar handwriting: "All's well here in the sticks. I never thought I'd be looking forward to coming back to the city, but I am. I even miss school, and my few friends there—like you. Anyway, I hope you're having a good vacation, (resting up from Ms. Newman.!!) I'll see you in a week, or so, I hope! Love, Zak (Hayseed.)" She studied the photograph, and read it again. She drank some more water, took two aspirin, got into her nightgown, and lay down, ears still ringing from the party. How did he get her address? She studied the envelope, and then lay it down on the bedside table next to her, for company.

She looked up at the clock—2:23, am. The New Year was already one hundred and forty three minutes old. She heard footsteps in the hallway, her father, and the door creaked open. "Good morning," he said, leaning down to kiss her on the cheek, smelling of the cigar he must have smoked at midnight— a ritual of her childhood. "Happy New Year," he said, and was gone.

Luck

Snow, cold, more snow. Great banks of old dirty snow and chunks of ice gathered along the brick sidewalks of the city. The afterglow of Christmas and New Year's faded, and then it was just cold and dull and gray.

School started up again—the familiar rhythm of classes, homework, the great teeming throngs of students—two thousand teenagers coursing through the hallways of the school. There were rumors about parties, an orgy that was supposed to have happened, and some kid carrying a gun around looking for revenge because someone slept with his girlfriend, as a Christmas present. But mostly it was the nerds in the hallway, and the clumps of geeky white kids looking like they crawled out from under some rock, the Haitians looking more and more American every day, betrayed only by their accents, and the beauty queens of all complexions with tight pants and shiny black shoes and breasts bulging over their shirts, and smart white kids from the AP classes, with their rosy cheeks and book bags and grand plans for their futures.

When Zak first saw Ivy in the hallway, after vacation, she had stopped and said, "Thanks for the post card. It was nice." And he was so surprised and eager to talk to her he couldn't think of anything to say, beyond the usual lame questions—how her vacation was—"Alright—nothing special,"—what she had done—"Not much, read a few books, went to a bad New Years Eve party."—Whether or not she was going to take Ms. Newman's class again for the winter semester—"Of course." She asked him about his time in Vermont, and Zak said, "Not bad. I saw a few friends, spent some time with my dad. Went skiing once. That's about it." He left out, for some reason, his drunken, New Year's Eve adventure with Jill Meyers. But when he had woken up the next morning, exhausted and vaguely hung over and happy, it was Ivy he was thinking of.

She was so pretty now—with her hair pulled back from her face with a blue barrette, her smile as she waited for Zak to say something else, but what? Ask her out, or something, and right on cue Yvonne appeared from nowhere, looped her arm into Ivy's, glanced at Zak and said, "Come on, let's go."

"I'll talk to you later," Ivy said apologetically, looking back at him as she was pulled away, back into her world.

But after these hopeful beginnings, he found it hard to find a moment to talk to her. In homeroom, she still came late, and Yvonne always saved her a seat, next to her. In Ms. Newman's class, she sat on the other side of the room, and Zak didn't know how to migrate over towards her without being too obvious, so he spent most of the class trying not to stare at her too much. After school, he would drift slowly in the direction of the square in the hopes of running into her, but he never did, and in the back of his mind was Nick's contention of some months before that she would never go out with 'white boys', anyway.

In the third or fourth week of the New Year, in the dull gray heart of winter, a crumb of good fortune fell his way. One day Ms. Newman asked them to get into groups, "with people you don't know," but when everyone just sat where they were, looked around dumbly, she told them to get back in a one big group and then "Count off by fours. This isn't South Africa, or Alabama, 1954. We need to mix it up a bit in here—let's see, twenty people, more or less . . . Why don't you count off by fives, just like you used to do in gym class." It took them a while to figure it out, but then they counted off—"one, two, three, four, five; one, two . . ." and Zak was "four", and before the counting had even gotten to Ivy across the room he could tell she was going to be a "one", but then the miraculous happened—when Ms. Newman's back was turned, this tall Spanish kid stood up and walked out of the room, with the result that Ivy turned from a one into a four.

"Four," Ivy said.

"Alright then", Ms. Newman said, "you are now officially integrated; this is going to be your study group for the rest of the semester. The ones in this corner, twos over there, etc." Introduce yourselves." The class groaned, looked at each other suspiciously, and then started getting up and drifting over to their groups. Ivy wearing a black shirt, new blue jeans, with pretty blue earrings, pretty eyes; Zak; a shy, gum-chewing Spanish girl; another girl named Valerie who was new to the class, but who Ivy seemed to know from church, or somewhere. Then Ms. Newman came over and made them introduce themselves, and the Spanish looking girl, from the Dominican Republic, said, chewing her gum. "Why do we have to do this?" and Ms, Newman said, 'because I'm tired of cliques. And by the way, I don't allow gum chewing in here. Sorry." The girl rolled her eyes, and walked to the trash can, swinging.

"I *thought* this was supposed to be a fun class."

"It is," Ivy said. The girl sucked her teeth and looked bored.

"And, oh yeah." Mrs. Newman said. "Please exchange phone numbers with your group. You're going to have to communicate." More groans, and a few protests, but they did it. "And now that you know who you'll be working with, you should all read the first chapter of our first book, *Their Eyes Were*

Watching God. The girl with the attitude didn't want to get in any group, said this wasn't "kindergarten."

"That's true." Ms. Newman said. "So maybe this isn't the class for you." Kids laughed. The girl sucked her teeth and sulked. Outside, through the window, Zak could see that it had just begun to snow. "Here we go again." he said to Ivy.

"I know." she said, "but at least it's pretty."

"It's all El Niño's fault." said Zak.

"El *Niña*." Ivy corrected him. "El niño is the cold one, niña's warm."

"Just like real life." Zak said, but she didn't get his little joke.

It snowed for three straight days. On the second day, when the snow was about a foot deep, they finally called off school, and Ivy stayed home in bed, in her pajamas, watching the snow drift down outside the window, gathering on the black branches, reading her book, all about some woman from down south named Janie: "It was a spring afternoon in West Florida. Janie had spent most of the day under a blossoming pear tree in the back-yard. She had been spending every minute that she could steal from her chores under that tree for the last three days. That was to say, ever since the first tiny bloom had opened. It had called her to come and gaze on a mystery." A vague impatience, a desire for something to happen: it sounded like her. After New Year's, Herman had stopped calling her, so much, and though it was a relief, she also felt slightly sad about it, like it was *she* who had messed up. It hadn't helped, later, when Yvonne had just shrugged and said, "It's your loss."

"What do you mean by that?"

"It's your loss, that's all—Herman's a great guy. He's good looking, cool, basketball star, he's going to go to a good school, play in the pros, be a millionaire, live in a big house . . ."

"He's five foot eight."

"So? I wouldn't worry about Herman, though. Plenty of girls like him. And he's not a nerd—not like that skinny boy you're always talking to."

"I've talked to him about three times in my life."

"Well, you should see the way he looks at you."

"Like how?"

"Like he's in love with you, or something. Maybe he hasn't heard we don't date White boys."

"We don't? Shit! I guess they forgot to tell me."

"Oh, so you *are* going to start talking to him?"

"No, but when I decide I don't think I have to take it before a committee first, especially one you're on."

"Then maybe what they say about you is true."

"What who says?"

"Everyone." Yvonne said, with a shrug.

"And what is that, exactly?"

"That you think you're better than everyone else—getting good grades, doing good in a school, your father's a big army man."

Ivy was about to answer but then, feeling her face flush with anger and hurt, turned and walked away.

"Don't get an attitude." Yvonne called after her. "I'm just telling you what everyone says, that's all. You're so *pure*." l

Pure? There it was again. Fuck *pure*. Maybe she should just let her grades slip and start smoking and start having sex on weekday afternoons, after school, going with bad boys and gangsta's that everyone seemed to find so appealing— give them what they wanted. Maybe her parents had spent too much time warning her about men, and what they wanted, and how they treated you afterwards.

The telephone had gone silent beside her—her brother playing computer games in his room, her parents away at work, Ivy home alone. She looked in the back of the book where they had written down their names and numbers. Monica, Maureen, Zak—225-4741. She picked up the phone and, before she had a chance to tell herself no, she dialed, then almost hung up, forced herself to hold on before a woman's voice answered.

"Hello."

"Hi," Ivy said. "Is Zak there?"

"No, I'm sorry, he's not. He's out skiing. Can I take a message?"

"Just tell him Ivy called, please—about our project."

"Alright, I will. Does he have your number?"

"Yeah, I think so. We're in the same study group."

"Alright, Ivy." she said. "I'll tell him."

"Thanks." She hung up, her heart beating in her chest. *Skiing*—in this? But Ivy was vaguely pleased with herself, this tiny act of rebellion, and lay back on the bed and read: "She was stretched on her back beneath the pear tree soaking in the alto chant of the visiting bees, the gold of the sun and the panting breath of the breeze when the inaudible voice of it all came to her." Ivy, too, was on the verge of falling asleep when she heard the familiar thump of her father coming in, back from a double shift on shift on the base; she heard him come up the stairs, then saw his face in the doorway. His black hat was covered with snow.

"Hey, Ivy." he said. "No school today?"

"Snow day. It's boring."

"Well, go outside then, it's not boring out there. Too exciting for me, in fact. I nearly got killed trying to get home from the base. It's a damn nuisance, this snow. I don't know why they invented it. But I better go shovel some. Do you know any CPR? They say the emergency rooms are full of old men like me, during snow storms. Cemeteries, too—full of snow shovelers."

"Don't talk like that Daddy." Ivy said, but her father, shovel in hand, clumping down the stairs, only laughed.

When Zak came in from skiing, covered with snow, lightly sweating, pink cheeked and happy, his mother was sitting at the kitchen table, as usual, with her books. "How was it?" she asked. "Great. I went down the river, up to the square, and all around. Your can ski down the streets."

"With the snow plows? Isn't that dangerous?" his mother asked, without looking up. "Go have a nice hot bath."

"I will." He was halfway up the stairs when her heard her say, "You got a call from someone—I wrote it down."

"Not Nick?"

"No. A girl."

"From home?"

"I don't think so. Iris, or Irene, or something."

"Ivy?" Zak said, pausing on the stairs.

"I think so."

"Did she leave a number?"

"She said you had it."

"I might." Zak said, and now something was thumping in his chest, and he was on his way up the stairs, and then the tub was running, very hot, and then he was undressed, his pale body slipping into the water and then he was in the bath, nearly burning himself, thinking about Ivy and why she might have called. He would have to wait a while—don't be too be obvious about it. Maybe it was something about their group, or the project they were supposed to be working on. He stayed in the tub as long as he could, his body pleasantly tired from skiing, then he dressed slowly, and then rummaged through his backpack for the book they were reading. He found it, but no phone numbers. His notebook, and there it was, written in purple ink, in a perfect, cursive script. "Ivy—624-5824." He paced around for a few minutes before dialing. It rang four times, and he was about to hang up before she answered.

"Hello, is Ivy there?"

"Yes." Ivy said sleepily. "She is. Hi Zak, how are you?"

"Fine. I just came in from skiing."

"So I heard. In this weather—are you crazy?"

"Only a little. But it's nice out—the city looks a lot better when it's being snowed on. What are you doing?"

"Not much—being bored. Reading that book for class. Dozing."

"You should go out and walk around."

"Not in this weather, thank you." Her voice sounded different on the telephone, and he pictured her lying down.

"It's pretty, though, and we got out of school, so I guess I shouldn't complain." She said.

"No, you should be happy."

He sat in a chair by the window, watching the few pedestrians outside, the occasional snowplow rumble by. As a child he had always loved the sound of snowplows, passing on the road as he slept. They talked about school, about the class, about some of the kids from school—Goldi-dredlocks, and Nick, and Yvonne.

"Don't mind her." Ivy said. "She's got an attitude."

"About what?"

"Life—it's a long story—I'll tell you sometime."

"Alright, don't want to pry."

Ivy laughed. "It's not that—I'm just tired of her, that's all. Plus, I'm bored as hell. Let's face it."

"Oh, so *that's* why you called me?"

"No," Ivy said, defending herself, "because I wanted to say hi, and we never get to talk in school, and I saw your number, and just decided to call—that's all."

"And we have to meet in our group, soon, for Ms. Newman."

"Don't remind me. But once this storm ends, we can plan."

"Good idea." Zak said, and just then his mother appeared in the doorway, making frantic gestures towards the phone.

"I think I have to get off the phone." he said. "My mother's making strange signals, like the house is on fire."

"Alright," Ivy said. "She sounds nice. I think I'll get up and help my father shovel, before he keels over or something."

"Call me later, if you want to."

"Alright." Zak said, "Thanks."

"My pleasure." Ivy said, and he could picture her half-mocking smile, and then she was gone, and he just sat there for a minute, staring out the window, his whole body felt like it was glowing.

"Thanks." His mother said, looking at him strangely, and he handed her the phone, hoping she wouldn't ask about who he was talking to.

But later at dinner, she said. "So who's your new friend?"

"A new friend, like you said," Zak said, and then added, "She's in one of my classes. Why?"

"Just curious—us mothers like to know these things, you know."

"Really? And why is that?"

"Because we're mothers, that's why—it's our job. She sounded nice, anyway."

"Phew", Zak said. "I'm glad you approve."

He went up to his room and lay on the bed, listening to the sound of snow, still lashing the window pane, imagining Ivy stretched out on her bed, a couple of miles away. He had felt strange and light, all afternoon, moving in slow motion, as if he was in possession of a small, precious secret that he must guard and protect from the world. 'Call me later, if you want to.' Ivy had said. He had waited until what seemed a good time—nearly eight o'clock, but it was a woman's voice that had answered, not Ivy's. She said she was still out, somewhere, with her father. "May I take a message?" she asked, her voice soft and slow, with a faint southern accent. "Just tell her Zak called, please."

"Alright, Zak," she said. "I will".

Cold

By February, the snow was still there, but the days had begun to lengthen, and there was a certain softness in the blue of the sky, and the snow seemed to melt more quickly, and at moments the long, cold winter seemed to be on the wane. After that evening Zak and Ivy often spoke on the phone, and sometimes she sat with him in homeroom. At night, if he hadn't talked with her all day he felt strange, and waited, hoping she would call, and if she didn't he would give in, finally, and call her, and hear how her day had been.

One day after school Zak and Ivy walked out of school together only to find Herman and Tyrone and a few other guys from the basketball team hanging out on the wall after practice. "Hi Herman," Ivy had said, and walked toward them, and there was a moment when Zak didn't know if he should wait for her or keep walking on his own towards the subway, but then he had heard Herman say, "Hey, Ivy. What's up Hayseed. Where are you headed?" and Zak drifted toward them.

"Home, I guess." he said, and then Herman and Ivy were talking, and Zak was just kind of standing there, and overheard him say, "So why don't you call me anymore?" and he could feel Tyrone and his friends watching him, and he was feeling stupid, just standing there, waiting, and finally he said, "I've got to go—see you later, you guys." And Herman said, "Later Hayseed," and Ivy looked over at him and said, "I'll talk to you later, Zak." And he walked away, feeling foolish and cowardly.

He had expected to hang out with her for a while, walk to the subway, together, at least, but he had crapped out on that now; everyone knew Herman still liked her, even though it was rumored he was seeing some pretty Dominican girl—a cheerleader for the basketball team.

He walked slowly in the direction of the subway, hands tucked deep into his pockets against the cold, hoping Ivy would break free and catch up with him. Though he had been trying not to smoke so much he felt a sudden, powerful urge to have a cigarette, and ducked into the smoke shop with the wooden Indian out front and bought two loose ones, a book of matches, and walked over to the pit, by the subway, where Nick Price was trying, in vain, to do some tricks with his skateboard on a patch cleared of snow; the board kept flopping up into a bank of snow, with Nick stumbling on the icy bricks. "Yo, Hayseed." Nick said when he saw him, smiling broadly. "Got an extra?"

"Payback." Zak said, and handed him one.

"Where've you been?" he asked. "I haven't seen you lately."

"Trying to study a little more—raise my B minus average, so I can get into college."

"Good idea." Nick said, smiling. "I got to give up the weed, myself—raise my C minus average. I'm losing my memory." He laughed. "Where's Ivy?"

For some reason the mention of Ivy irritated him.

"I don't know." he lied.

"A fine woman." Nick said, shaking his head at the thought of her. "A very fine woman, as a matter of fact."

"Yes, it is a nice day." Zak said, his nerves wearing thin. "We're just friends, anyway. She's a lot smarter than I am—she helps me in school."

"Cool." Nick said, nodding, tugging on his beard, thinking.

By the time Ivy got home that afternoon, it was almost dark, a weak winter light bleeding in through the window. She was still irritated with herself for the way she had handled it, for not telling Zak to wait for her, or just keep walking with him. Why hadn't he waited—scared off, probably, by Tyrone and his friends staring at him. There was something unclean about the whole thing, and she wanted to talk to Zak, or hear from him, make sure everything was alright between them. She felt like calling him, but didn't really want to talk to his mother, or leave a message. Outside, it was already dark, and a long evening was yawning before her. She should be doing something else with her life—but what? Until ninth grade she had run track, and a couple of years before she had been in the choir at St. Paul's, but practice was two nights a week and church lasted almost all day Sunday, and against her mother's protests she had quit, and hardly even went to church anymore. She checked the dial tone of the phone, took her book out of her bag, took off her skirt, pulled on her pajama bottoms, and crawled in under the covers to read, or to sleep, restless and vaguely disappointed in herself.

And now Herman was talking to a beautiful Spanish girl, little Miss cheerleader with a beautiful woman's body, who was probably giving him what he needed to feel like a man. But how could you regret loosing something you had never really wanted in the first place, anyway? That too, like many things in her life these days, was a mystery.

The next morning, as usual, Mme. Maillard was wearing a black cashmere sweater and tight red pants, revealing more than usual of the perfect shape of her "derrière." Even the girls watched as she drifted up and down the aisles, pausing now and then, and tapping someone on the shoulder. "Monsieur," she would say. "Comment ça va?"

"Très bien, Mme Maillard, et toi?"

"Et 'vous,' you mean."

Ivy wasn't very good in French and always felt nervous as the teacher drifted around between the desks. And sure enough, as she passed, she tapped Ivy on the shoulder and said, "Et vous, Mademoiselle Whitman. Comment ça va, aujourd hui?"

"Très bien, merci, Madam?"

"Mademoiselle, s'il vous plait. Et quelle est votre couleur favorie?"

Ivy could feel herself getting nervous.

"Mon couleur . . . favorie . . . est bleu." she said slowly.

"*Ma* couleur." Mme Kirkland corrected, and then added. "Très bien. Merci."

After that, she knew she was off the hook for a while, and so slid into a pleasant state of rest, daydreaming, wondering what was so urgent that Yvonne had to tell her? She had accosted her before class, and told Ivy she had to tell her something—immediately. And she still hadn't seen Zak yet—he hadn't called her, and wasn't even in homeroom that morning, and worried he was mad at her, or something.

By the time class was over, Ivy was almost falling asleep in her chair, and when the bell rang she went to her locker and found Yvonne waiting. "Let's get out of here." she said.

"I've got to study." Ivy said. "We can walk around the block."

They had hardly gotten outside, into the cold blue light of the February afternoon, when Yvonne said, "It's about Herman."

"Let me guess." Ivy said. "He's seeing some Spanish cheerleader—Ms. Body Beautiful with long eye lashes and booty beautiful."

"Who told you?" Yvonne said, stopping in her tracks, and looking at Ivy.

"Everyone who gets a chance—like I'm supposed to be upset or something."

"You're not?"

"No, why would I be? We're still friends, I still talk to him, like yesterday."

She looped her arm through Ivy's and tugged her along while they walked. "Anyway, some of the Spanish guys aren't too happy about Herman taking their woman. They're talking about jumping him—if Herman wasn't on the basketball team, they would have done it already."

"Oh, God—great." Ivy said. "Here we go again—West Side Story. Anyway, they're not Spanish; they're Dominican. Spain is in Europe—the Dominican Republic is in the Caribbean, next to Haiti."

"Thank you, Professor. They all talk Spanish, right? Then they're Spanish. Anyway, Herman better be careful. If you had gone out with him he wouldn't have this problem."

"What problem? Next subject, please—this one is kind of old."

They had turned the final corner of the block and were coming back out in front of the school, walking through the motley throng of students that had just been released for the day.

"Why can't Herman find a Black girl, anyway—always chasing after someone else's woman. First he likes you because you're light skinned, and then he has to . . ."

That's when Ivy stopped walking: "What?" she said.

"You heard me. Besides, you're smart and pretty and going to be a doctor one day and you live in a nice house and your dad's a big army man and . . ."

Ivy started walking again, eager to get away from this talk; they had made it back in front of the school when she turned and said "Why are you such a bitch these days?"

"It comes naturally," Yvonne admitted. "Anyway, that's not what I wanted to tell you."

"No? You have more good news?"

"Yeah—I think I'm pregnant. I'm almost a week late."

"Congratulations. I'll buy you a stroller."

"It was an accident."

"Haven't you heard of birth control, Yvonne? It's amazing what science can do. They've been practically throwing condoms at us since we were twelve."

"We're not all so sensible as you. And in a moment of passion, it's hard to remember."

"Oh dear. Passion—I forgot. You're probably just late. You better go get checked anyway."

"I'm too scared to, but it might be O.K., having a baby, right?"

"You're kidding, right? You're sixteen years old."

"Seventeen."

"Well, go talk to the nurse—maybe they have a morning after pill."

"I would need a month after pill."

"Great. Anyway, call me tonight and tell me what she says," Ivy said. "I've always wanted to be a godmother."

Ivy hurried along the empty halls and ran up a flight of steps towards the library. But she had lied to Yvonne—her study group was not supposed to meet that day. Instead, she had come back here because in the back of her mind she had half hoped she might find Zak here, where they usually met for their study group. She was afraid he was mad at her, or felt she had blown him off the day before. But he wasn't in the library, and wasn't wandering around the halls. He was probably in the pit with Nick, smoking. She went back outside, and there was a steady stream of kids walking towards the gym—a basketball game. She didn't want to go home, didn't want to study. Herman had been complaining she never came to see him play, and she found herself walking in through the heavy red door, past the frozen trophies of golden athletes, in through another set of doors, to the gym, full of parents and students a few teachers sitting in the bleachers. All the colors were alive, vibrant, and it was pleasantly warm in there—a hothouse of adolescent energy.

Ivy walked halfway up in the bleachers and sat down by herself, watching the teams warm up. Herman was there, looking different in long, baggy shorts—collecting the ball, taking a few dribbles toward the hoop, laying it up and in with the practiced, casual grace of the schoolyard, loping back and around to the end of the line. And there were the cheerleaders with their pom-poms and their yellow and brown uniforms and their short, swirling skirts, running out onto the floor on tip toes, jogging around the center circle, going through their routines. It all seemed quaintly old fashioned to Ivy, like a scene out of the fifties—except here there were two Black girls, one Asian, and one Hispanic one—a pretty girl with a beautiful figure and long, silken hair—who must be the famous Sonia, the Spanish beauty queen Herman had found when Ivy had failed him on New Year's Eve.

"Hi Ivy." someone said, and sat down beside her—Miss Goldi-dreadlocks, from class—Heather.

"Hi," Ivy said, and realized she didn't know the girl's name.

"I didn't know you liked basketball?" she said.

"I don't." Ivy said. "My friend's always complaining I never come to the game, so I thought I better."

The game had just started—ten boys sprinting up and down the floor. The other team was from the suburbs, somewhere—four white kids with crew cuts and one black guy—their star player, it seemed—everybody's hero because he could throw a ball through a hoop.

The crew cuts had jumped off to a surprising lead, and were running around in a state of high excitement, bumping chests and raising their fists, and acting like they were about to win the NBA championship. And then there was Heather, beside her, trying to make friends. Every time her head moved, the beads of her locks clacked together, and even this soft sound bothered her, though she didn't know why. Maybe it was because she seemed to be doing it on purpose, to draw attention to herself.

"Let me get out of here." Ivy said, unable to summon any interest in the spectacle. "I think I'm going to be ill—they look like the marines or something."

"You're leaving already?"

"Yeah, I'm not much of a cheerleader."

"I'll talk to you later." Heather said. Heather—the one who had been dancing with Zak that night. On her way down the bleachers Ivy looked over at the bench and caught Herman's eye as he stood listening to the coach, getting lectured. He nodded when he saw her, and gave a kind of weak smile, as if to say, 'Yeah, we're getting our asses kicked, but don't worry. It's in the bag.' Then Ivy looked over at the cheerleaders and, sure enough, Miss beautiful Spanish bobby socks was looking up at her with a slow, glacial stare, her eyes fixed on Ivy until, suddenly, she spun away, her jet black hair fanning around her head in slow motion, like she had been watching too many shampoo commercials.

Outside, it was snowing again, soft, large flakes drifting down through the windless air. So what if Herman liked light skinned girls, and now Spanish? Where was Zak, and why hadn't he called her the night before? And now Herman had seen her, sitting with Miss Goldi-dredlocks at the game, and she had left early, and Spanish beauty queen gave her the look of death on her way out.

And now it was snowing again, in this endless winter, covering even the streets, where the cars moved like large, lumbering animals. A bunch of Chinese—Asian—kids were walking along before her, talking and laughing in a strange and unfamiliar language, the girls looking pretty with snow gathering on their heads, like a painting she had once seen at the museum. Did it snow in China and Japan? Why were Asian girls so thin—narrow waists and hips that seemed to tilt slightly forward? And if everyone was supposed to be the same, genetically speaking, why did Spanish girls have wide hips, and black girls have bigger butts than everyone else? And why was she feeling lonely, suddenly—Ivy the beautiful, Ivy of the many friends, smart and pretty with a sharp tongue, if she needed it, bound to go to college and get her picture in the paper and do the right thing by everyone, date the right guys, make her Grandmother cry with joy and pride?

She turned off the sidewalk to cut across the campus—it was beautiful there, still and quiet, the sky slowly falling in soft, swirling flakes of white that landed on the warmth of her smooth, brown skin, melting, gathering on her eyebrows and the tufts of hair that came out from under her hat. Ivy, of the soft and beautiful eyes, her mother's eyes, her father's laugh. She stopped for a minute and listened to the sound of snow falling—a soft hiss, like the background radiation of the universe they had talked about in science class, the audial residue of the big bang.

The college kids were shuffling back and forth across the campus with their bundles of books and worries, or were off in the rooms, making love to each other, like you were allowed to do in college, naked on a winter afternoon. In a couple of years she would be one of them—maybe not here, but somewhere else, far away, where it didn't snow; for a minute she could sense her own future stretching out before her, vague and uncertain. And afterwards? Married, with children? She couldn't picture any husband, nor herself at any sink, day in and day out, like her mother. But her mother worked, too, until recently, as the librarian at the local elementary school. What would she become—lawyer Ivy, in a nice pin striped suit? Doctor Ivy in white? None of the above.

She kept walking, slowly, now, and then she thought she heard a voice behind her—the far off sound of her own name. She stopped, but resisted the impulse to look, listened and waited. "Ivy!" she heard someone say again, and there was a certain urgency in the voice, and still she waited, and suddenly knew who it was, heard the footsteps behind her, muffled by the snow, and knew this was what she had been waiting for all along. Still, she did not look— heard "Ivy" one more time, and then someone's arms reached around her, surrounded her, and only then did she turn and look up into his soft blue eyes. "Where have *you* been?" she asked him. His face was flushed pink, and he was still panting from his run, his head giving off steam like smoke.

"Looking for you." Ivy looked over at him to see if he was smiling, and noticed, on his upper lip, the faint hint of a moustache. His eyes seemed bluer than usual.

"I was at the game, you know." Zak said, "But you didn't see me—you were too busy talking to Heather."

"Oh, so you know her name?" Ivy said.

"Ah . . . yes."

"Heather, Haystack—nice." Ivy said, teasing. "I forgot you knew each other—now I remember—your dancing partner."

Zak laughed, wondered if she could actually be jealous. "I was missing you." he said.

"You were?" she asked, but didn't wait for an answer. "Why weren't you in homeroom?" she asked.

Zak opened his mouth, and showed his teeth. "Only one cavity. Want to see?"

"No thanks."

"I thought you were going to call me last night." Ivy said.

"I tried, but it was always busy. Besides, I thought your phone might be tapped."

"No, I fell asleep with the ringer off." Ivy said, watching his face. "Sorry. And how come you took off, yesterday, anyway?"

"Took off?" Zak laughed. "Well, no one exactly encouraged me to hang around, and I started to feel kind of dumb standing there, waiting for you to finish up with Herman. It doesn't matter now."

"Where are we going, anyway?"

"Anywhere, but here."

"Let's walk—it's nice out." Ivy said, and they started off across the campus and as they walked she was aware that a sudden lightness had come over her, a sense of relief in the knowing that all was still O.K. between them, and he wasn't mad, and that he was beside her, now, and it didn't feel at all strange when he looped his arm through hers and pulled her closely to him as they walked, toward nowhere, their feet making a pleasant crunching sound in the snow.

Secret

In the days and weeks to follow Ivy kept to herself, mostly, and her books, protective of the small secret that lived inside her, now, or hovered somewhere between the folds of her sweater and her skin. What was it she was hiding—she didn't even know. Nothing, really, had happened between them, but she saw him every day at school, and she would call him at night, or he would call her, and she would lie on her bed talking to him, with her books and stuffed animals and other artifacts of her childhood. If she didn't talk to him she felt strange, like part of her day hadn't happened, and went to sleep with a strange sense of urgency, wanting to get to sleep quickly, so the next day would come, when she would see him. She couldn't tell Yvonne she was talking to him and she was even afraid what her father would say, given his general ambivalence about boys. He had nothing against them, he always said, as long as they didn't bother him, or try anything with his daughter. And then he would laugh, his big throaty laugh. It didn't matter anyway—they were just friends, as they say.

"Good news." Yvonne's voice said on the answering machine one evening when Ivy got back from school. "No need to worry. Call me if you get a free moment." Ivy didn't appreciate the insinuation, but was relieved to hear Yvonne would not be adding to the wealth of babies at Central High School. Next, it was Herman's voice. "Thanks for coming to the game. If you had stayed til the end you would have seen us stomp those boys. I scored twenty points, or so. Anyway, thanks for coming. I'll talk to you."

Recently, Herman himself seemed to have dropped his attitude, either because he had given up, or because he had started seeing, they said, Sonia, the Spanish beauty queen, head cheerleader, and her brothers weren't too happy about it. Her image that stuck in her mind—the cheerleader with the jet-black hair that swirled around her head, like a shampoo add on TV. She was beautiful, it was hard not to admit, with her olive colored skin and large dark eyes, and fine body, somewhere between Ivy's and Yvonne's.

Then, one Monday morning Herman came into school with a black eye and a small cut on the side of his face, and his hand in a large, white cast. He didn't want to talk about it much, but a few people had been there when it happened, or claimed they had been, and few foggy and debatable details had begun to seep out and swirl around the hallways and classrooms of the school, like smoke: a party at someone's uncle's house across the river on the east side of the city; Herman and a couple of his friends arriving late, with Sonia on his arm. But there were some other kids there, who didn't go to Carver Central, didn't care that Herman was Mr. Basketball, only knew that Sonia was very beautiful, and one of them spoke to her in Spanish, and learned that she was from the Dominican Republic. A couple more beers, more talk, the sight of Herman's arm around her narrow waist, and one of the young men asked Herman why he couldn't leave "our women alone?"

"Because she's not *your* woman," Herman said, a response that didn't help matters. A few more unpleasantries were exchanged, their bodies assumed a taught, coiled look, and it wasn't so much a first punch that was thrown as a cuff, a slap on the side of someone's head, followed by a push, then a punch, and then suddenly there was an excited knot of young, male muscles, fueled by testosterone, in the middle of the party, shouting, swaying, girls screaming, falling down, scratches, a stray kick or two. The police were there with astonishing speed, for once, and for his trouble Herman ended up with a black eye, a cut just above cheekbone, and a broken left hand, which felt like someone had accidentally dropped a cinder block on it. Someone's head, he'd discovered, was surprisingly solid and heavy, like a large chunk of ice or stone, and when you punched it, it hurt back—which was more about physics that he had ever managed to learn in Mr. Nicolosi's class. As he left the scene of the party, under the gaze of two policemen, he noticed that the floor was littered with flecks of red, like blood, only it was the broken off fake fingernails of the girls, including Sonia's. There was much debate in the school about whose fault it was.

Herman was embarrassed about the whole thing, and it was clear he would not be able to shoot a basketball for a while, and it was also possible he could be dropped from the team for fighting, being out late on a weekend, and various other infractions.

"I feel bad for him," Yvonne said one morning in homeroom. "But that's what happens. He never should have been messing with their women—that's what happens." Ivy just rolled her eyes.

"Not this again," Ivy said.

"You would say that," Yvonne said, nodding toward Zak. "We know where you're headed. And as for Herman, Black girls aren't good enough for him."

"He can talk to whoever he wants."

"What do you think, Zak?" Yvonne said. "Don't you think people should stay with their own kind?"

"Geesh," Zak said, "The pressure's on. Yeah, I think people should only go out with people who are the same height, shoe size, and IQ—preferably their own brother or sister. Life would be a lot simpler that way." Ivy smiled, and Yvonne gave him the look of death, wondering if she'd been insulted. She sucked her teeth, and went out the hall.

"Touché." Ivy said. "Where'd you get that smart mouth?"

"Even a broken clock is right twice a day." Zak said.

Ivy laughed. "Not bad, Haystack. You made it up yourself?"

"No—it's my grandfather's saying. It's about one hundred years old."

"See you later?"

"I imagine."

That night as she helped her mother make dinner, chopping up carrots, Ivy asked if she could have her study group over sometime, to work on this presentation they had to give.

"As long as you give me advanced warning—I don't want anybody talking about our messy house."

"I thought you told me not to worry about what people say—just live your life, and do the best you can."

"Sure, but you don't want to give them any ammunition, in the meantime."

"I hear your boy busted up his hand." Ivy's father called from the other room as he thumbed through the paper. He was sitting in his usual chair in the pool of yellow light cast from the old, standing lamp beside him.

"He's not 'my boy', for one thing." Ivy said. "And he hurt his hand because these Spanish guys didn't like him showing up at a party with a Dominican girl, that's all."

"Not surprising. Even the Spanish people don't like us, for some reason—think they're better than us, never mind taking their women. Everyone's always looking for someone else's head to step on—I guess that will never change, at least not soon."

"It will change when people get tired of being stupid." Ivy offered.

"Not talking about me, I hope."

"If the shoe fits . . ." Ivy said softly, and her mother nudged her in the ribs. "No, Daddy. Of course not. *Other people. Not us.* We're different."

"People aren't very good at changing, as far as I can tell." her father said, "You take those White folks, for example . . ."

"Mom, can I change the broken record? I think we've heard this one a few thousand times before."

Her father chuckled. "That's true. But some things bear repeating."

"Can we please talk about something *else*?" Ivy's mother suggested, laying down her fork and going back into the kitchen. "I think I'm losing my appetite."

"The truth doesn't make for good dinner table conversation?" her husband said happily. And then he slowly rose from his chair, raised his hand into the air and pronounced, rather more loudly than necessary. "And we're still in slavery today!!"

He looked slowly around the room, eyes wide open, slapped his knee, and then burst into a long, rolling laugh, like a train passing under the house. "I love it when they say that." he added, coming back to himself. Even Ivy smiled.

"I guess they don't really know what real slavery was, or what my grandparents went through afterwards, sharecropping themselves to death—seven children, only four of them making it to the age of twenty. My mother was one of them—working in somebody's kitchen for another fifty years or so."

"Can we eat, please?" Ivy's mother said, coming back into the room with a hot plate of food. "All this talk is giving me a headache."

"By all means," he said. "That is why we are gathered here, I believe, my beautiful family. Where's that son of mine, anyway—always with his nose in that computer. And as for you, beautiful," he said, looking over at Ivy, "Don't worry about a thing. I hear through the grapevine that there's someone calling you every night. You tell him to come around for inspection, some time, so we can see what he looks like."

Ivy looked over at her mother. "Thank you, Mrs. Grapevine." she said.

"Can we eat, please!!" she said.

"Yes Mam!" Mr. Whitman said, giving a mock salute. "Let us break bread. And praise God for all of his blessings!!"

"Or hers." Ivy muttered softly to herself.

Lead

The excitement about Herman busting up his hand and missing some basketball games was overshadowed when, on an otherwise pleasant and rather warm winter afternoon, just as the sun had slid down behind the rooftops of the city, and a dog barked, and some birds settled into a nearby trees, and squawked, a recent non-graduate of Central High was shot outside the city youth center, next to a small pine tree by the basketball courts. The dead boy's girlfriend, whose photograph Zak recognized as someone from his neighborhood, was also shot in the shoulder, but they said would be okay, though it was not clear if she would regain full use of her arm. The paper described it as "another senseless shooting" when an argument that started in the gym over a pick up basketball game between two boys, aged seventeen and twenty, spilled outside, and before anyone knew what was happening they both pulled out guns, fired off blindly at each other, and then everyone ran: only the two victims, who were sitting on a nearby bench, stayed behind in the late afternoon sunshine, slumped to the ground, the girl screaming, bleeding in the snow. The young man, named Hector, died there; Christina, hysterical, screaming her boyfriend's name, was taken off to the hospital. A couple of hours later workers from the city arrived to clean up the snow, stained a bright scarlet by their blood, and within a day or so small shrine had been erected by his friends and family on the small evergreen tree where he had died, with candles and Teddy bears and photographs of the happy couple in their prom dress, from the spring before. The word around the school was that, in the spring, she would be she was having his baby.

On his walk back from school one day Zak took a detour to look at this place where, a couple of days before, a boy his age had died: a couple of candles flickered weakly, and well worn Teddy bears sat stoically in the cold, and now and then a couple of kids would show up, mill around, add a flower or card, and then shuffle away. Back in Vermont, car crashes were the popular means of teenage death, and occasional hunting accident, but never murder— well, almost never. But it was too cold to hang around, and so Zak, with an eerie, sickening feeling in his chest, walked slowly home under a low, threatening sky, the color of lead.

At school for a couple of weeks the conversation shifted to teenage violence, and guns, and what could be done about it, and a special counselor was hired to help students deal with the death of their recent classmate. One of the boys thought to be involved in the shooting was picked up for questioning; the other—a drop out from Central—was nowhere to be found, though Florida and Texas were mentioned as places he might have fled to. The City Council attempted to pass a resolution banning the sale and distribution of firearms within the city limits, but councilor Al McGuire, backed by the National Rifle Association, led a movement against the motion, citing the constitution and its famous clause, "the right to bear arms".

"Even when our school children are dying in the streets?" he was asked by an angry parent.

"The firearm in question," Mr. Lopez countered, "was acquired illegally—not at a store."

It was pointed out that virtually all guns were initially acquired at a store before they began their strange and meandering journey though the sweating hands of anxious teenagers, but he did not respond. In school, a few teachers made the attempt to talk in their classes about violence, and what to do about it, but then the students' conversations slid back toward more cheerful topics, like who hooped whom over the weekend, and who was pregnant, maybe.

"When your number's up," Jamaul was saying one day after school to Herman and Yvonne and Tyrone, "it's up—that's all. If a bullet's got your name on it, or some germ carried by some queer dude, there's nothing you can do but chill, that's all."

"They say you can get that AIDS shit from women, too." Tyrone said. "But I don't believe it—gay guys, or needles, mostly."

"Oh, no?" Yvonne said. "I know a few girls here you might want to talk to. I plan on living a long time, myself—no raincoat, no booty, that's all."

"Yeah, right," Tyrone said. "That's what you say now, but when the moment comes, you'll be singing a different tune."

"Don't worry—you won't be there to find out." Yvonne said, and then laughed happily, like music. She was wrapped in a giant black coat stuffed with feathers, and she looked like the incredible hulk, only prettier and brown.

"You got that right." Herman said. His hand was wrapped in an ace bandage.

"We'll see about that." Tyrone said. "We'll see." And then he added, unnecessarily, "Not all of us can date Spanish girls. Give me a nice Black girl, big booty, like Yvonne here, any day."

"Dream on." Yvonne said, but smiled at the compliment anyway.

Just then, as fate would have it, unlucky Zak emerged from the front of the school, heading home—he forgot to take the back door. When he saw them his first impulse was to stop and turn around, but it was too late.

"Yo, Hayseed." Tyrone said. "Where's your girl? I saw you walking in the square the other day, and you were walking mighty slow, like you had no where to go."

"Whose girl?" Zak said, a current of dread running through him.

"Don't play that," Tyrone said. "you know who I mean."

"Little miss college girl, that's who." Yvonne offered.

Zak could feel his face turning red. Charged at last. "Oh, Ivy!" he said sarcastically, "I don't know where she is, actually."

Yvonne said. "I see you two in homeroom, talking and whispering, playing footsy, probably."

"Shut up, you two, would you?" Herman said. "Give him a break—what are you bothering him for? Hayseed's cool. He can talk to whoever he wants."

"You, too?" Tyrone said. "You're defending him, and he stole your girlfriend?"

"Shut up, man." Herman said.

Zak still felt the need for clarification: "She's not my girlfriend, actually."

"Don't worry about it, Hayseed." Herman said, "You can talk to whoever you want. It's not like, 1940, or something."

"What's wrong with *you*?" Yvonne said.

"What's wrong with me? I got my face punched because I showed up at party with Sonia. Then I wrecked the whole fucking basketball season because I punched him back. If one of those guys had a knife, I'd be dead, now, too. For what?"

"You should have had one yourself." Jamaul said.

"Fuck you."

"What? If you're hand wasn't broken, I'd kick your black ass myself."

"Kick, or kiss?" Herman said.

"This is kind of fun, guys," Zak said, "But I have to go. Thanks for the chat, though. I enjoyed it. See you later, Herman."

"Later, Zak." Herman said.

"Punk." Jamaul muttered, and they watched him as he walked away. His walk had changed, slightly, slowed down, taken on the rolling cadence of the city.

"What about you, Herman?" Tyrone asked—"you hooped her yet, or what?"

"No, and I'm not planning on it either, so shut up, would you?"

"Oh, I forgot—Spanish girls don't give it up until their wedding night—just like that other one you wanted. Man, you must be hurting."

"Fuck you." Herman said softly, almost to himself.

"Let's go." Yvonne said, and Herman just sat there as they walked away, laughing.

"Shit." He muttered to himself, and could barely muster the energy to walk over to the gym and watch the last game of the season which, to everyone's surprise, they easily won without him.

By the time he reached the campus of the college, Zak's face was still hot from a mixture of embarrassment and anger. He had always been able to talk his way out of trouble, sidestepped the tough kids back in Vermont who tried to hassle him in the boys room, made fun of him because his pants were too short, or because he was in the AP class with all the nerds, but he had never had to put up with shit like this. As he came into the campus, among the milling college students, drifting along the snow lined paths, the low clouds parted and for an instant a soft yellow sun shed its milky light across the campus and Zak stopped a moment, closed his eyes and tried to forget what had just happened. He walked up the steps of the large brick church, and then went around the side to the small courtyard where, in the afternoons, he had taken to meeting Ivy on a small stone bench someone had cleared, where the sunlight fell in the late afternoons, where they could sit, away from the din of the school. Here, nobody knew them, and they could sit and talk before they headed home. There was always a pleasant sense of anticipation, of waiting, knowing she would come. And then there were footsteps behind him, and then a fragrance of her, and then her warm weight setting down on the bench beside him. "Hello, stranger. Been waiting long? Sorry I'm late." she said, "As usual."

Zak looked over at her pretty face, the slender arc of her eyebrows. In the soft light of the sun, her skin was a pale, lighter shade of brown.

"Not really. I was held up by our fan club—they told me to say hello to you."

"Who?" Ivy said, touching his arm. In Zak's family, people seldom touched, but in the middle of a conversation Ivy would reach out, in an unselfconscious way, to hold onto his arm, or shoulder, or knee.

"Your best friends—Herman, Yvonne, and what's his name was the worst—Jamaul, that dickhead fuck."

"Goodness," Ivy said. "Bad words!! I guess they did upset you. What did they say?"

"Just some dumb jokes about you being my girlfriend, or something, and then they started bothering Herman about being with Sonia and . . ."

"God," Ivy said, "They never stop."

"It's not your fault."

"I know but, she's supposed to be my friend—or at least used to be."

"Until *I* stumbled along."

"No, it started before that—she's always had a problem with me about something."

"Like what?"

"Being a nerd, studying too much, having both parents around, still married, thinking I'm 'all that,' being light skinned, having straight hair, sort of—you name it. Her father disappeared when she was five, and her mother's a slut. She thinks I think I'm better than everyone."

"She's jealous."

"Maybe. She's kind of dark, and has a big butt . . . probably lost her virginity when she was twelve. Stuff like that."

"Ah well, let's change the subject. It's nice out. I'll walk you home, just like the movies."

"Oh, great." Ivy said. "You can carry my books, too."

"Alright." Zak said, pulled her up, and hugged her, imagined he could feel the warmth of her emanating through their clothes. "Maybe spring will be early this year."

"Don't get your hopes up. It's only February." Ivy said, and they walked, his arm looped through hers.

Storm

For several days Dick Webb, the buffoonish weather forecaster had been pointing to a large "system" pulling itself together, somewhere in the gulf of Mexico—a swirling mass of clouds, a high pressure system, a low pressure system which, if all went according to plan, would meet somewhere off the coast of South Carolina, converge, and start a slow steady climb up the coast and arrive in their city sometime in the late afternoon on Thursday.

"They're never right." said Zak skeptically. "It probably won't even snow."

"I wouldn't be so sure." his mother said, "they've been right all year." She was sitting at the kitchen table in front of a pile of books, wearing glasses. It was a little hard for Zak to get used to this new version of his mother as a student. "Your friend called by the way." she said distractedly.

Although he already knew the answer, Zak asked "Which friend?"

"The young lady—Ivy. She didn't leave a message, just to tell you she had called."

"Alright." Zak said softly, "thanks." He had hoped to slip out of the room without a discussion, but it was too late.

"How is she, by the way?"

"Fine," Zak said, "the last time I checked."

"And when was that?"

"Oh, a couple hours ago, in school."

"She's very pretty, by the way."

Zak looked at her. "How do you know?"

"I saw you walking together in the square—I honked, but you didn't hear me."

"That's nice: my own mother spying on me."

"I was *not* spying—I just saw you. You looked happy—so did she."

"Well, we're just friends, if that's what you're working up to."

"I'm not."

"Anyway, if we ever actually went out for a date, whatever that is, there'd probably be riots or something."

94

"Why is that?"

"She's not supposed to be hanging around with 'white boys'."

She paused and looked over at him. "I thought your generation was beyond all that, now?"

Zak rolled his eyes. "Yeah, me, too, until Herman got punched in the face, and Yvonne started hassling Ivy for hanging around me."

"And what about the other kids—the White ones?"

"I don't really know that many, besides Nick and Heather. Nick's always stoned, and Heather likes Black guys, anyway. Then there's all the A.P. kids who walk around in a little clique and talk about where they're going to college. And there are like no Black or Spanish kids in those classes—though there's a few Chinese, or Cambodians, or something. I heard some girl over on the east side got thrown out of her house for having a Black baby. Now, they're getting married, I hear. It will be a very small wedding."

"And what about *her* parents?"

"What about them?"

"What do *they* think?"

"I don't know, mom—we're just friends, remember? Why, what do *you* think?"

"About what?" she asked. Zak rolled his eyes. "Me, chilling with a Black girl?"

"I have no real problem with it . . . at your age, anyway. When you get older, maybe, there are other issues . . ."

"Like what?"

"Well, children, for example."

"What about them?"

"They say mixed children are confused, sometimes—aren't fully accepted by either group. They don't know who they are."

"*Most* kids don't know who they are, as far as I can tell."

"You do."

"Yeah—I'm a country bumpkin. That's my identity."

"No you're not. Anyway, all I'm saying is, when you get older, there are other things to think about besides who makes you happy—family, society, stuff like that—but that's all a long way off, I'm sure."

"Yeah, sure mom—and that's what you were thinking about when you married dad?"

His mother looked at him and gave him a weary smile. "No, actually, but maybe I should have. We all married too young, back then. It doesn't matter much, at this point, anyway." He sensed in her a desire to steer the discussion back unto safer territory. "She sounds very nice, and I'm happy you have a good friend, that's all. To be honest, I didn't even know she was Black?"

"What?"

"I mean, she didn't *sound* Black on the phone?"

Zak rolled his eyes. "Geesh, Mom. I'm going to have to report you to the PC police. And how does a Black person sound, by the way—ghetto, and all that?"

"You know what I mean, Zachary. Don't give me a guilt trip, please—more than I have already."

"Alright, Mom. I'll let you off the hook, this time."

"Thank you very much," she said, looking flustered. "If I don't finish this paper, I'll flunk out and we can all go back to Vermont and live happily ever after." She looked down at her book again, which Zak took as an invitation to drop the subject.

Then he remembered what he wanted to ask her: "What was that case that happened when I was like ten, or something—this man killed his wife and two children over in Brattleboro, or something?"

"Oh, yes." His mother sighed. "I remember that. He was White, and she was Black—from down in Massachusetts, somewhere. They had moved up to work at the college. One morning, he said he got a call from someone, saying he should go check on his family. They went, and they found that they were all dead—strangled. Later that day, they arrested him, and later he got convicted—the trial went on for years. It was in and out of the papers."

"Why did he do it, they said?"

"Who knows? He cracked, obviously . . . at the time, people thought the pressure might have been too great—being in an interracial marriage, or something. Other people said he had a girlfriend, money problems."

"But husbands kill their wives all the time, these days. It's like the national sport, or something. So who's to say it was because she was Black?"

"There were notes found at the scene, apparently—something about 'blacks and whites don't mix.' I think that's why people were talking about it. But that was years ago—if you're interested you could probably look it up. Some people, even Rev. Jones, thought he was innocent, and still do, maybe."

"And where is he now—the husband?"

"In jail, somewhere, I believe. Why are you so interested?"

"I don't know—I just remembered it for some reason, but couldn't remember the details."

"It caused a lot of friction in town at the time—people weren't prepared for this sort of thing. And no one wanted to think it was some crazy, racist group, like the KKK or something."

"Maybe it was."

"I don't think so. The evidence was pretty compelling. He had scratches on his face, and she had a broken fingernail . . . stuff like that."

"I see." Zak said. There was a knock on the door. "Jesus, there's my boyfriend again. Nick—I like the guy, but . . ."

"Tell him you're busy."

"No, I'll hang out for a while—nothing else to do, except homework."

"Well, get it all done, OK?"

"I will, when I get back."

There he was—a thin face surrounded by a wispy yellow beard: old man winter himself.

Outside, it was colder than he expected, and a great mass of high gray clouds like an enormous battle ship, was drifting up from the south. "Snow." Zak said, stuffing his hands into his pockets.

"Cool." Nick said, sparking up a cigarette.

"It's fine with me, too." Zak said. "One giant blizzard, and then we'll be ready for spring. Give me a cigarette, would you? I'm too young to quit."

Jones

For some reason, Zak started to do better in French that quarter, though he didn't know exactly why. Mme. Maillard seemed to like him, for one thing, and he took a kind of pleasure in decoding these unfamiliar sounds, words, and sentences, as they opened a door on a distant and benevolent world, far from the clattering confusion of the school. France, if the illustrations in his tired text book were to be believed, was a land of neat and narrow streets, bakeries on every corner, men with well clipped mustaches and pretty women carrying umbrellas, waiting for rain.

And of course, there was the teacher herself, with her alluring body and pretty pale face lightly touched with freckles, and her lips, each day a different shade of red, sounding out the mysterious sounds of this unfamiliar language. It was rumored that she was 'friends' with one or two of her students, had taken them over to her house for candle lit French dinners. Strange sounding, but maybe true. He liked the class, also, because it was the last one of the day, and he knew that he would be leaving afterwards.

But this particular Thursday, he was vaguely nervous: after school, he was supposed to go over to Ivy's house, for a study group with one other girl, preparing an oral report they had to give the following week, on some writer, or other. "Now you get to meet my parents—my mother, anyway." Ivy had said.

Outside, it was cold and gray, and as he walked toward the square he wondered if the study group would be cancelled because of the much predicted storm. He had hoped to see Ivy after school, to talk to her, but had a feeling he wouldn't, and as he walked slowly in the direction of the square something cold kissed his face, and then again, and then he could see, high against the black branches of the trees, that it had started to snow. He walked faster, clutching in his pocket the crumpled piece of paper on which she had written her address—memorized, in case he lost it—243 Fairweather Rd, second floor. They owned the house, she had already explained, rented out the first floor to some graduate students from the Divinity School.

He was early, too, and so decided not to take the subway after all, but walk: across the frozen campus, through the square, and then along the avenue, through a part of the city where he had never been: past a pet shop, a "cooking college", an Indian restaurant, a fragrant and stale smelling bar. The snow was falling a little harder now, and had begun to turn the sidewalks white, and wispy, sinuous trails swirled along the street in the wake of passing cars. He always loved this moment, the beginning of snow, and it evoked in him some deep and happy memory of his childhood.

He was hungry, had forgotten to eat lunch, and when he got to the end of her street, he was still early and stopped into a corner store to buy some round little peanut butter crackers that he liked. A couple of old men sat at the counter, nursing their coffees, and talking, and two boys, a couple of years younger than Zak, where buying some candy and chips at the counter. As Zak looked around, grazing for food, he heard them talking to the proprietor—some discrepancy about the change they had gotten back. The man behind the counter—tall and thin and with hair combed back on his head in the style of Zak's grandfather, counted it slowly back to them. "Oh, OK." one of them said, nodding. "Sorry about that."

"No problem." the man said. "I know it's confusing—I get confused myself, here, sometimes, and I've been ringing up candy bars for thirty years, now—going on thirty two, actually."

The two boys moved around behind Zak, and as they left the store a gust of wind and snow came swirling in. Zak was paying when one of the men, the larger of the two, his skin gray like old newspaper, glanced around the store and they said, with a casual clarity, "These niggers are something, aren't they?"

His friend chuckled, Zak could feel his face flush, and then the man behind the counter looked up at them. "Jesus, Jim, cut it out! I've know those boys since they were kids—I know their parents, they're customers of mine—them and a lot of other people." He didn't look at the men directly, but went about his duties with nervous, agitated motions, shaking his head.

"Alright, Joe." the fat man said, as though he had heard all this speech before. "Relax. Whatever you say. Don't have a heart attack. We'll see what you have to say in a year or two when they come back and rob you."

"Well—I've been robbed twice—once by knife, and once at gunpoint—and both times they were white guys, alright? Probably your nephews, or something. I hear one of them's locked up."

"Relax, Joe, would you? It's just a word. They use on each other all the time—so what's wrong with us saying it, too?"

"It's not the same, you asshole. You know that. You think I'm stupid? In any, case, I don't like it, and it's my store, so . . . that's it."

"Whatever you say Joe." the man said, sliding off his stool. "You're the boss. I'm gone. Put it on my tab, would you—two coffees and a donut. I'll be getting paid next week, hopefully."

Joe did not answer, but turned and wrote something on a tired slip of paper he had taped to the wall. The two men left, heads bowed against the cold. In the heat of their discussion, he had forgotten entirely about Zak, who was still standing there waiting to pay.

"Sorry, son." he said. "I didn't even see you there. Eighty-five cents, please. I don't know what's wrong with these guys. You'd think they would change. I'm sorry you had to hear that. I can't have that kind of talk in here. It's a family store. I have all kinds of people in here—not just Black. Spanish, Chinese. I won't lie to you—I used to use the word myself, in the fifties—everybody did. But you know, we changed—most people, anyway. What are you going to do? They upset me. I don't need that. I should retire. I'm too old for this."

Zak wanted to say something him, but what? "Maybe next time they'll think twice." He offered.

"That would be nice, but I doubt it. When they get out in their truck, or back at their houses, they'll keep it up, I promise. They can't change—it's too late for them." he said wearily, and sat down at the counter, waiting for business. "Other people, maybe, but not them. And then they can't even pay for a coffee and donut." He shook his head, wearily. "What's your name, by the way?" he asked. "I'm Joe."

"I'm Zak."

"Are you new in the neighborhood?"

"No, I'm going to see a friend down the street, do you know the Whitman's?"

"Oh yes—Ivy. I've known her since she was a baby. Pretty girl. Very nice people. The father's in the Navy, or something."

"Army, I think." Zak said."

"Oh yeah, they come in here all the time. Very nice people. Tell them I said hi. And come again, if you're in the neighborhood."

"I will." Zak said, and went outside, his face burning. Even his cookies had taken on an unpleasant aftertaste. He threw the last one over someone's fence; he did not hear it land, silenced by the snow, frozen until spring, when some lucky chipmunk would find it.

He was no longer early: the snow was an inch or two deep, and a few flakes had gotten into his shoes, slowly melting there. He followed the numbers upwards—121, 123,125—to 133, a well kept green triple-decker, the same color, it occurred to him, or a scarf Ivy sometimes wore and, if it was cold enough, wrapped around her head. He had never seen her in a hat, that he could remember. He walked slowly past the house to the end of the block, stalling for time, and then walked back to it, up the stairs, and rang the bell. He could hear it ringing above, and then footsteps coming down the stairs. It wasn't Ivy who opened the door, but an older woman who looked a little like her. "Hello," she said pleasantly, "you must be one of Ivy's friends, from school."

"I'm Zak." Zak said, shaking her hand.

"It's nice to meet you, finally—I'm Ivy's mother." She was younger that he had imagined, with Ivy's eyes and high cheekbones, her hair touched with gray. "Come on in." she said, walking back up the stairs. "I'm afraid Ivy isn't even home yet, but she should be any minute now."

"I'm early, I think." Zak said. "It's snowing hard, now."

"A big storm, from what they're saying." She led him up the stairs into a warm, pleasant room suffused with a soft yellow light. "Have a seat in here— she should be home soon. Are you hungry? Do you want anything to eat?"

"No thanks, I'm fine." Zak said, but in truth those peanut butter crackers had not squelched his hunger, and the exchange in the store still sat uneasily in him, as though he had brought something sinister, unclean into the house. He took out his book, but then just sat there, looking around at the photographs on the wall: Ivy, smiling shyly, with braces; a black and white picture of her young looking parents in wedding clothes, at a family reunion. There was a coil rug on the floor, a sleeping cat in a chair. As he sat, it occurred to him that he had never been in the house of a Black person before. How could that be?

It reminded him of the homes of his friends back in Vermont—small, cozy places where they would hold out against the winter, waiting for spring. Ivy's mother reappeared with a dish full of cookies. "Have a cookie. I don't know where that girl is." she said. "So you have to work on an oral report?"

"Yes, on Langston Hughes." Zak said.

"That should be fun."

"I don't know much about him." Zak admitted, and then heard the door open below, thumping, and then the sound of someone running up the stairs. "Hi mom!" Ivy said, and came into the room, cheeks flushed, her hair capped with snow, melting before their eyes.

"You're not mom." she said to Zak, and laughed, "Have you been here long?"

"Five and a half minutes, or so." Zak said.

"So you're counting?"

"And where have you been, young lady?" her mother said, giving her a kiss. "Leaving your guests to wait for you."

"I got held up at school. Ms. Newman wanted to talk to me about something. Sorry I'm late. Did Isaura call? She's supposed to be coming."

"Not yet. And probably won't make it in this weather."

"Why don't you work at the dining room table." Ivy's mother suggested. "I cleared it off for you."

Zak followed her into the other room, and they sat at a dining room table so shiny he could see the vague outlines of Ivy's face reflected in the polished wood. She was wearing jeans, and a light brown sweater, and perfume he did not recognize.

"Where's your other friend?" her mother asked, looking out the window, where the snow was falling harder, still, lashing against the pane.

"I don't know." Ivy said.

"I'm surprised even you made it, Zachary." she offered.

"He's from Vermont, Mom. This is, like, a normal day for them."

"Well, not quite. But they don't call off school very much."

"Ivy tells me your mother is here studying for a year or two?"

"Yeah," Zak said. "She's going to get a Masters in Education, and maybe a doctorate after that."

"I'm envious. And then she'll be going back to Vermont?"

"I don't know." Zak said. He was bracing himself for a question about his father, but mercifully it never came. "We'll see. I think she—we, actually—are starting to like it here. Vermont's kind of dull, unless you want to raise cows, or work at a ski area."

"It's the *whitest* state in the country." Ivy offered. "And I don't mean snow."

"Oh, Ivy. Always thinking of something smart." her mother said.

"True." Zak said, enjoying this moment of collusion.

"Well, I'll let you two work. Let me know if you want anything."

"Thanks, Mom," Ivy said, and from her book bag pulled out a sheaf of books and spread them out across the table. "I don't think the rest of our so called group is going to make it."

They wrote up a biography, found a couple of his poems to read aloud, and made up some questions to provoke class discussion. Ivy made him read a poem aloud five times, critiquing him each time for clarity and intonation.

"Louder." She kept saying, "and slower—more feeling."

"Hey, I'm a Vermonter. We're suppressed."

"Repressed, you mean."

"Oh, yeah, that's it—repressed." he said. The poem was about a girl named Susanna Jones, who wore a red dress: "When Susanna Jones wears red/ Sweet silver trumpets, Jesus".

"Like this," Ivy said, and stood up and acted it out, standing with her hand on her hip, transforming herself, for a moment, into a night club singer. As he watched her read, he was pleasantly aware of the shape of her, the deep curve of her waist, the swelling of her breasts, the theatrical way she moved when she read the poem. "Maybe *you* should read this one." Zak suggested.

"No, because it's about what this boy feels for this girl . . ."

"Yeah, but." He tried again.

"Better." Ivy said. As they worked, their knees sometimes knocked under the table, and all of the nerve endings in his body had gathered there, on red alert, like soldiers sent to the front line. Was she aware of this, he wondered, or did she think his knees were the table legs, or something?

Zak was also aware of feeling happy—the warmth of the house, the soft yellow light, the presence of Ivy's mother in the kitchen, the radio on low, the sound of her voice singing a few lines as she worked, the snow lashing against the windows. It was still falling, through darkness now, and he was enveloped by a sense of safety, shelter he did not feel in his own house anymore. "Do you think you should call home?" Ivy's mother said, in the doorway. "Your mom might be worried about you." Was this a hint it was time for him to leave?

"I'll call her before I go." Zak said. But he would have rather stayed for dinner, and then curled up with the cat on the rug and slept there, all night, and then walked with Ivy to school. But they had finished their project, more or less, and dinner was getting ready, and Ivy's father was expected soon, and Zak had an inclination to get out of the house before he returned home. "I'd better go," he said to Ivy when they were alone, "or I really will have to spend the night."

"You can if you want," Ivy said, and quickly added. "You'll have to sleep in my room. Just kidding—my father would have a stroke."

"I wouldn't want that." Zak said. "The stroke, I mean."

"Do you want to see my room?" she said, and he followed her down the hall and led him into a soft and pleasant kingdom of pink and blue, a few stuffed animals on the bed, a beautiful old quilt as a bed spread, a couple of posters of beautiful, well formed women on the wall, one of Michael Jackson, when he was about fourteen and still looked beautiful, before he had started messing with his face. On the table beside the bed sat the blue phone, and answering machine blinking with its captured messages. That's where she would be when he talked to her at night, sometimes, her slight and lovely body held only in a bathrobe, or nightgown. "So now you know everything about me." she said.

"Do I?" Zak asked, lingered for a moment longer, taking it all in. "It's a nice room."

"Here, look at some of my pictures." Ivy said, and he sat beside her on the bed—Ivy as a baby, in a stroller, her grandparents on the front porch of their house, out in the country, friends and family, Ivy in a sequin dress one New Year's Eve. Their arms were touching now, her warmth pressing towards him, his desires held in check by the audience of teddy bears, guardians of her childhood, that were all staring at him, waiting for him to make the wrong move.

"And this is when I was ten." Ivy said, "We were living in Virginia Beach, and went to the sea for a holiday, and . . ."

"Ivy." Her mother said, coming into the room. "It's almost six. The news says it's going to keep snowing, so I think Zak should get going soon."

"Yes, mother." Ivy said. "One second—we're almost done."

Her mother stood there for moment, looking at her, and went back down the hall.

"I better go." Zak said, "I don't want to make anyone nervous." Ivy rolled her eyes. "Yes, the head nun has spoken."

He stood up, and let his hand land for a moment on her back. "Thanks."

"For what?"

"Showing me your stuff."

"Anytime. You're sure you can make it home alright?"

"If not, they'll dig me out in the morning."

"Don't joke. Seriously, you'll be alright?"

"Yeah—I like it, actually. I'll be home in half an hour."

"I'll call your mother," Ivy offered, "and tell her you're snowshoeing home."

"If you want. But I'll be alright." Zak was heading down when they heard the door opening below—a click, a stomp of feet. "Uh-oh," Ivy said. "Head rooster alert." And then her father's feet came clumping up the stairs.

"Ah, a welcoming committee." he said happily, brushing a hat of snow off his hair. He was a solid, handsome man with a pleasant, amused expression on his wide, open face, his hair touched with gray.

"Hi Dad." Ivy said, and leaned over to kiss him.

"Hi beautiful." he said, and then held out his hand to Zak. "Nice to meet you, young man. I'm Ivy's father."

"I'm Zachary." he said.

"We were working on a project together." Ivy explained.

"Glad to hear it. Please forgive my war clothes—I'm straight from the base. Let me go change."

"Well, thanks again." Zak said to Ivy's mother.

"You're welcome, Zachary. Come again. It was nice to meet you." He went down the stairs with Ivy close behind him.

"Be careful." Ivy said and then added, "Call me when you get home."

"Alright." Zak resisted the impulse to try to kiss her goodbye, winked instead, and then went out into the blizzard, running through a formless world of wind and snow, happier than he could remember. Ivy went up the stairs, bracing herself for an onslaught of questions.

"So *that's* your famous study group." her father said cheerfully when he came out of his room, reaching over to capture Ivy in his arms. "I thought there were four of you. What happened to the other two?"

"Lost in the blizzard, I guess."

"And *he's* the one who's been calling around here every day?" he said, shaking his head. "He's a tall glass of milk, alright. I guess I don't have to worry about *him* stealing my baby. He'll be lucky if he isn't blown away on his way home, with this wind."

"That's not nice," Ivy's mother said and then added, "actually, I kind of liked him. There's something kind of sad about him. Where was it you said his father was?"

"Back in Vermont," Ivy said. "they're separated. I think she came here to get away, and go back to school."

"Lucky woman." Ivy's mother said, then added under her breath, "The school part, I mean."

"What, dear?" her husband asked.

"I said, 'terrible weather'." And then she turned to Ivy. "Zachary is welcome here any time he wants. He's a nice boy."

"Easy, now." her father said, settling in with the paper. "I don't mind him dropping in now and then with his school books, but I'm not quite ready to feel sorry for him just because his parents don't get along."

Ivy rolled her eyes. "I'm going to study." she said, wanting to cut off this particular line of commentary, but she could still hear her father chuckling, "Yup, he's a tall glass of milk, alright. I hope he makes it home."

Ivy closed the door and lay down on the bed and listened to the wind whipping up the snow outside, lashing in against the window panes, the low, muffled growl and rumble of the passing plows. She lay her hand down on the bed beside her, in the place where he had been sitting, aware that she had not wanted him to leave.

No school tomorrow, and she would not see him, then. When would this winter ever end? She had liked the ease with which he had talked to her mother, absorbed her father's blustery energy, the shy way he had smiled at the bottom of the stairs, touched her back. And why had his knee kept touching hers under the table, and why had she moved hers closer to his instead, like a good girl, moving it further away.

"Well, we know about *her*." She could hear one of her aunts saying, and then adding, with a kind of withering disdain, "I buy Black, myself, if you know what I mean." They generally spoke with disdain about those who had "crossed over", sucking their teeth, and muttering, as if they had drifted over into some other world, beyond her reach, never to return.

She turned on her radio, but only love songs came out—too corny to listen to. She turned it off, preferring the sound of the wind and the snow. Maybe it was he who had left her the Valentines card in her locker, signed "a friend". She had assumed it was Herman, or someone else, but the handwriting didn't quite match. She had been too afraid to ask. He had continued to surprise her, in small, unimportant ways. She had never been able to picture him in her house, yet here he had been, sitting at the kitchen table, talking amiably with her mother. Too many thoughts that would not stop, she heard footsteps in the hall, the door creaked open, and her mother's warm presence was beside her. "Dinner's ready, honey." she said, her southern cadences seeping into her voice.

"What are you thinking about?"

"The foul and inclement weather."

"You like him, don't you?" she asked.

"Who?" Ivy asked, trying not to smile.

"Nice try. You know who—that boy, Zachary."

"Mom, can I eat later? I'm not hungry."

"Alright, baby. I'll save you some. But do your homework," she said, and the door closed quietly behind her.

Silence

The storm, as it turned out, was the worst of the last decade, or second worst—the weatherman couldn't decide which—two feet in twenty-four hours, no school for two days. Zak had spent the first day shoveling—his mother's house first, and then her car, and then a couple of other peoples' cars, and then he helped an elderly woman who lived across the street. It was a jolly scene out there on the street, and for the first time since they had arrived people were outside, talking and shoveling snow, pushing cars, leaning on their shovels, marveling at the storm. For once, everything had slowed down, gotten quiet, cars had given way to people, walking everywhere along the suddenly narrow paths between the high banks of snow.

The day after the snow storm he had called her, left a message "just to say hello", which Ivy had listened to curled up in her quilts and Teddy bears, but she did not call him back. Something about what her mother had said, and the little smile she had given her, and implication that it carried. They were friends, that's all, but she remembered his legs touching hers, under the table, and she was aware that she would have usually moved hers away, but did not feel like it this time, and even, trying not to be obvious about it, returned the light pressure he seemed to be giving her.

She wouldn't call him: if they were just friends—she didn't need to talk to him every day. And even though Yvonne was a bitch, sometimes, she still sort of missed her, her talk and her calls and the little whirlwinds of mischief and trouble that always seemed to be swirling around her. It was difficult that night, falling asleep without having talked to him all day, and she wondered if she wasn't being a bitch, too—the way girls are supposed to be: if you like someone, ignore them, don't give them too much attention, the conventional wisdom went. In the morning, he left another message, his voice sounded strange to her, not mad, exactly, but not happy, either. "Hello, hello," he said, "Earth to Ivy, Earth to Ivy—hope you didn't get buried, or anything . . . anyway, this is Zak, just calling to say hello. Pick up if you're there . . . pick up, pick up . . ." Then there was a pause, and his voice trailing off. "Ah, well. Talk to you later," and then the dial tone.

Zak, for his part, felt a strange cloud of apprehension surround him, a kind of loneliness, missing her, then wondered why she wasn't calling him back. The evening had been so sweet, and he was now tormented by the picture of her room, and her in the middle of it, curled up on the bed, the warmth of fragrance of her body wrapped in wool, flannel, fleece-cotton, a quilt made of feathers—and in the middle of it all, her, her warm body, her soft brown eyes blinking back at him as he lay her beside her. Dream on, as they say. He tried to not think about her, lying there, naked under her clothes. Maybe he had scared her off. He needed to get away from her, from the phone that was not ringing, from his mother burrowed up with her books, and took a long, pitiful walk by the river, along a path packed in the snow by other walkers, but he could not get her out of his mind, and thought about walking straight to her house, and running up the stairs and into her room to see what she was doing. But instead, he looped back through the square, looked for Nick, in the pit, then wandered home.

There would be school in the morning, surely—she would see him then, Ivy thought. She would go to bed early, and in the morning, she would go to school, and she would see him, say hello, and . . . cool. What's the big deal? She was brushing her teeth when she heard the phone ring, and she ran to get it, but by the time she got there the person had hung up, and left no message. Maybe it was him again, or Yvonne—she would never know. He'd call back; she'd see him tomorrow, anyway. Whatever. Forty eight hours—that's all. It's normal, if you're friends. But she couldn't sleep, and reached for the phone once or twice, but then didn't, and then did. By the time she gave up, and stopped fighting with herself, and she called and he answered on the fourth ring, his voice sounded weird and distant. He had already given up. "Zak?" she said softly. "Did I wake you?"

He paused and then said, "No, I was just sitting here, wondering if you'd fallen off a cliff, or your father had forbidden you from calling me, or something. It's been like, two weeks since I heard from . . . talked to you."

"Two days, actually." Ivy said, and then added, "It only *seemed* like two weeks."

"So what have you been doing?"

"Lying around, waiting for this stupid winter to be over with. Thinking about stuff."

"And what did you think?"

"That I missed you, and I don't know why I wasn't calling. I'm stupid, I guess."

There was silence from the other end. "No you're not." He said, and Ivy could hear in his voice that he'd been hurt, but was trying not to be.

"That's good to know," he said, "because I was about to come over to your house and break the door down. Or go off with Nick and start a cult."

Ivy laughed. "Don't do that. Next time I act stupid just come over and tell me. I'll let you in, and you can get mad at me in person." At the sound of his voice she could feel the blood rush back into her body. She wanted to say something, by way of apology, but what? "I can be kind of dumb, sometimes."

"You and me, both. You'd better sleep, and me too, now that I know you're still alive."

"Alright." Ivy said. "See you tomorrow?"

"Yes, please. Sweet dreams."

"Alright . . . goodnight." She said, and was about to add a pitiful *I'm sorry*, but he was already gone.

Sellout

Two days later the sun came out, a warm, spring sun, and all the snow began to melt, drifting off in streams to pools, seeping back into the warming earth. Within a week, almost all the snow was gone, except for a few dirty piles that would take weeks to disappear.

By the first week of March the air had grown softer, and the trees had already started to show signs of life, branches touched with yellow and red, buds forming. Outside the school in the park, kids gathered in usual groups, the blue smoke of cigarettes rising up like the smoke from little campfires.

Zak and Ivy, for the most part, avoided this happy scene after school, preferring to steal away and meet at the familiar place on a bench, where nobody knew them, or cared, and they could sit for a while and talk, or set off on one of their slow, meandering walks through the city, often ending at the end of the street near Ivy's house. Zak would stand and watch her walk halfway down the block to where, at the same fire hydrant, she would always turn to wave goodbye and, even from this distance, he could see her smile. And then he would set off on his own meandering walk towards home.

But it was true that Ivy missed her old friends, missed talking to Herman, and even Yvonne, and one day made a point of waiting in school a little longer, and then coming out the front to where they usually sat, and there found him, in the usual place. She smiled when he saw her. "Hi Herman," she said.

"Hi, Ivy," he said, "where have you been hiding?"

"Not hiding—just busy, that's all. How about you?"

"Alright," he said, "now that basketball's over, and my busted hand is getting better, I can stop feeling like fool for punching that guy." He held up a rather weak and pale looking hand that looked like a dead fish.

"How is she, by the way?" Ivy asked.

"Couldn't tell you," Herman said. "She won't really talk to me, since our little problem. I think she's under orders from her family not to talk to me. And if I call her house, they hang up on me."

"That's cold. I'm sorry to hear that. People are dumb—let's face it."

"True. And how you doing? I hear you're been spending a lot time with Zak." There was no malice in the question, no hostility.

"We're friends. We talk a lot, hang out sometimes."

"That's cool. I won't pretend I don't have feelings for you, but what can I do? I love Sonia, but . . . who knows." Herman looked kind of pitiful, sitting there, with his broken hand and no beauty queen to be with, no basketball, the school year running out like water down the bath tub drain. And here he was, giving her his blessing.

"And how are your grades? Are you doing alright?"

He was just about to tell her, but here came Yvonne and Tyrone, right on schedule. Yvonne was looking a little more hoe-ish than usual, her body pulled into tight black pants, leather boots, her hair straightened and then shaped into swooping curls, her lips a strange reddish blue.

"Hi, Herman." she said, then smiled at Ivy thinly and said, "Hi, snow girl."

"I told you not to call me that." Ivy said.

"Oh, sorry. I forgot," Yvonne offered glibly.

"Snow girl? Why don't you lay off, Yvonne?" Herman said. "What's the problem? What are you giving her a hard time, for?"

"What's this—the new interracial dating club?" Yvonne said. Herman looked away, staring vaguely across the park, something seething inside him.

"Cut the bull, would you?" he said, and slid off the wall where he had been sitting.

"Easy now, basket-boy," Tyrone said, stepping toward him.

"You, too, gangster? Shut up, would you?"

"No, you shut up, nigger, before I kick your black ass back to Africa," but Herman just kind of smiled and said, "No, that's alright. I'm cool just where I am." Then he turned back to Yvonne.

"What's up, Yvonne. I thought you two were friends."

"We were, until she started kissing up to Ms. Newman, thinking she's all that, hanging out with wi . . ."

"What?" Ivy said, her face burning now. So now the truth was finally coming out—just because of Zak, because she got good grades, and didn't didn't say 'nigger' every other sentence, she was a sellout.

"Yvonne," she finally managed to say, her voice quavering. "So now you've finally got it said—what you think of me. You come over to my house, eat my mother's food, flirting with . . ."

"I'm not good enough for your mother's food?"

"Chill, would you two?" Herman said, standing up. Yvonne had taken a step toward Ivy, Ivy had taken a step back, and he stepped in between them.

"And now she's going to beat me?" Ivy said. "This is fun."

Suddenly Ms. Newman appeared from the front doors of the school and, walking toward them said, "What's going on you guys?"

"Ask your star pupil. Come on Ty—let's get out of here." Yvonne strode away and Tyrone, glancing back, dutifully followed. Ivy watched as a pigeon swooped down from a nearby tree, and hopped down onto its own shadow, wobbling along the ground. She could still feel her heart beating.

"Yvonne's jacked." Herman said.

"About what?" Ms. Newman asked.

"Everything, it seems like. I'll talk to you later, Ivy. I've got to get out of here, before someone else tries to jump me. I really don't need all this aggravation."

"Thanks, Herman. See you later."

Ivy's face flushed, her complexion deepened a shade or two toward scarlet. Ms. Newman slipped her arm around her shoulder and said, "My car's in the parking lot. Let's take a drive."

"Alright." Ivy said, and followed her to her car.

Down by the river, large chunks of ice were floating by like ships, and a few ducks drifted in the water not far from the bench where they sat. It had felt strange to be driving around with a teacher, but it felt better here, out in the open, looking out over the river in the warm yellow light. A few joggers thumped past, leaving damp footprints in the soft, sun warmed soil. Ivy told her the whole story coming over, for what it was worth—becoming friends with Zak, Yvonne's catching an attitude, culminating with the little scene in front of the school.

"She called me 'snow queen'." Ivy laughed.

"What's that supposed to mean?"

"I'm not really sure." Ivy said, "Maybe that I'm cold and white. I don't think it's a compliment."

Ms Newman chuckled. "I guess not." She was wearing red tights under her black skirt, and her knees kept sliding out between the folds of cloth. Her hair was done up in small braids, and her face was neither young nor old, but pretty. "Well, you've got a lot going for you—you're young and smart and motivated, you have a good family, and . . ."

"Yeah, I know," Ivy said. "And Yvonne's got a single mom, and her dad took off when she was a kid, and she lives in the projects and has a big butt and all the guys want to fuck her—I mean, sleep with her—and I'm Miss Goody Two Shoes with penny loafers, hardly ever kissed a guy before, and now I'm hanging with White boy, and so I'm a sellout, just like they always said I was."

"That's not exactly what I was going to say—but, close enough."

"Sorry."

"None of that really matters. She's still probably jealous of you. I'm not really sure where Yvonne's headed, and neither does she, and that's part of the problem. And, ah, one more thing about Yvonne, that I should probably mention, off the record, of course: she's a bitch." She paused and laughed. "I don't like the word, much, but they must have invented it for a reason. I know, because I *can* be one too, but I try not to be. Some people like it. Maybe she'll change, maybe she won't. Most people don't, unfortunately. God forgive me, but some women, and men, just are—sorry."

When they stopped laughing, they sat in silence for a while, watched a flock of ducks swoop down from somewhere and glide onto the water with a swoosh. A fat man with bare pink legs jogged by. "Keep on running, honey," Ms. Newman said quietly. "you'll get there."

"So you *are* friends with, ah, Mr. Zachary?"

"We talk, we go for walks, corny stuff like that."

"He likes you?"

"As a friend, anyway."

"That's all?"

Ivy smiled slightly, and paused. "Probably not all."

"And you?"

"I like him." She said, and wondered if she should admit she found him attractive—his shyness, his sad blue eyes, the way his clothes hung loosely on him and looked like they wanted to fall off, but never did, the way he touched her now and then and pretended it was all in innocence.

"To be honest, I never thought I'd be spending so much time with him. It's like, it just kind of happened."

"Life is like that—sometimes, things just happen. It's not like going to the super market and picking out a friend. They find each other. And if it got more serious, you wouldn't have a problem with it?"

"You mean, aside from losing all my friends and being disowned by my father? No—not at all."

Ms. Newman laughed. "What about your mom?"

"She's cool, I think. My dad would probably go into cardiac arrest—he's always talking trash about White folks this, White folks that. You know—the usual party line."

"And Zak's parents?"

"I don't know. He doesn't talk about them much. His Mom sounds nice on the phone—she knows about me, but we haven't met yet. I don't know about his father. He's not around."

"Well, people have a way of getting used to things . . . they'll get over it. You don't meet that many people in life you get along with, and when you do you can't just push them off because they don't look like your daddy. And you can't live other people's lives for them—they've had their time, made their own choices, but it's your turn, now. And as for your Dad, I've met him. He may be saying a lot of this out of habit, because that's what he's used to. Most people don't change until you give them a reason—or a push. He may be more open-minded than you think. He seems like a big hearted person to me, once you get past the bluster."

"He is." Ivy said, looking off across the river to where the sun had slid behind one of the spires of the college, casting them in shadow, and the warmth gave way to a sudden chill. A few ducks and geese were paddling around in the water. They stood up and walked back into the sunlight towards the car.

"You're a beautiful woman," she was saying to Ivy, "and a lot of people are going to be wanting you to be who *they* want you to be. But you can't—so you're going to have to live your own life. The people around you will adjust. And if they can't, ah, well."

"I won't tell my parents that."

"Good idea."

They stood up, and walked along a path on the edge of the river, the packed earth turned soft and damp under their feet when Ivy blurted out, "And who's *your* boyfriend?"

"Now that's a whole other story." Ms. Newman said, and chuckled. "I generally keep it to myself, but, between you and me and the nearest bed post, I gave up on men a while ago. I was married once, but, well, I am with a woman now—a White one at that. I have to keep it to myself, or I might lose my job. People don't like lesbians teaching their children, for some reason. The school board might think I'm corrupting the youth."

Ivy was kind of shocked herself, but tried not to show it. "That's interesting." she said.

"You had no idea?"

"Not really—I guess I never thought about it."

"And *you* should have been there when I told my parents—that was fun! I thought they we're going to disown me, and they probably did too. Within a year, I was taking my lover to Thanksgiving. As my grandmother used to say, 'You carry your own hide to market'."

Lover, Ivy thought, trying out the shape of the word in her mind. Was she Zak's *lover*? She forced a weak smile. "And what does that mean, exactly—carry your own hide . . ."

"Everyone has to live their own life. No one can do it for you. We all have to make our own choices, and sometimes people don't like them. But that's their problem, not yours. You have to separate the two. Life is hard enough as it is." She paused and watched her face. "But I'm rambling. I'm beginning to sound like a teacher. I'd better let you go. Your parents will worry, think you're off with 'that boy' somewhere."

Ivy laughed. "Actually, my parents are pretty cool. I think my dad just says things out of habit, sometimes, because it sounds good." she said.

"That's good. And if you ever want to talk, give me a call at home—my number's in the book, believe it or not."

"Alright." Ivy said, and leaned toward her and gave her a hug goodbye, and then watched Ms. Newman as she moved quickly away, not looking back. "I'm with a woman now." she had said. So that's why she dressed kind of strangely, almost like a man, sometimes. If the kids at school found out, they'd go ballistic, writing graffiti all over the bathrooms. She could see it now—"Ms. Newman's gay!!"

She could loose her job? Even now, in 1994? She would keep the news to herself, or just tell Zak—he wouldn't care. She continued along the river, cool blue shadows alternating with patches of sunlight—spring, then winter, then back to spring again—a slim, pretty girl walking alone, her eyes turned amber, her skin glowing like copper in the rays of the setting sun.

Spring

Zak found a phone booth on the corner and quickly dialed the number that, in recent weeks, had burnished itself into his mind like a poem: 624-5824. He always dialed with a vague sense of excitement, anticipation, fear that she would not be there. And when he spoke with her on the phone, each night, he always imagined her in the magical kingdom of her room, lying on the bed among the pillows and the teddy bears, in the soft light, a pallet of pink and blue, and the thought of her there alone, without him, filled him with a kind of longing, a need to see her, talk to her—a sweet kind of pain and desire and need he had never felt before. Since he had been to her house, several weeks before, he had been haunted by the memory of her room, the watch-guard bears, the pictures on the wall, and there on the bed, Ivy, bathed in the soft light and mysterious fragrance of her self, waiting, he liked to think, for him to call, or arrive.

It rang three times before the machine came on, her voice sounding slightly older than she really was. "Hello, this is Ivy. I'm not available right now, but if you want to leave a message, please do so after the tone."

"Hi, Ivy." Zak said to the machine, "I was in the neighborhood, and I thought I'd give you a call to see if you were home, and . . ."

"Zak?" Ivy said, as the machine beeped off.

"That would be me."

"Where are you? You sound strange."

"Down by that corner store, at the end of the street."

"What street?"

"Your street?"

"Why?"

"I was eating a Twinkie, but I can't eat both, and was wondering if you wanted the other one. Plus, I'm waiting to see if you'll come out for a walk. It's nice out finally—you know—spring, I think it's called."

There was a pause, and then she laughed and said, "Alright. I'll be down in a minute. Don't go anywhere."

116

She hung up, quickly pulled on a sweater, then shoes, and looked out the window, sunlight filtering through branches of the maple tree that was touched with a blurry, reddish shadow of spring.

"Bye, mom." she announced to her mother, who was sitting in a chair reading one of Ivy's books.

"And where do you think *you're* going, young lady?"

"Out," Ivy said and, realizing that was not going to fly added, "For a short walk."

"And with who if I might ask."

"With *whom*." Ivy corrected her. "Zak, actually."

"And since when do you two just go out for walks?"

"Since he asked me to, about one minute ago—if I'm allowed to, that is."

"Just be back in an hour or so, that's all. Your father will be home soon."

"Alright, Mom." Then she was gone, quickly down the stairs, the door swinging shut behind her. Her mother sat still in the chair, looking out; through the window, open to the warm spring afternoon, she could hear the sound of her daughter's footsteps running down the rust red bricks of the city. In a year, she would be eighteen, then she would graduate, and be off to college, somewhere, but where? Already, she dreaded her absence, her going away. What would it be like without her—her empty room, long afternoons at the end of which she would not come home. Maybe she would go back to work, then, teaching, or something, as she had done before Ivy was born. But how? She was no longer young. And where had Ivy gone now, looking so pretty and happy? She closed her eyes, and must have dozed off as the light in the room grew slowly dimmer, as it did in the late afternoons, as she woke to the sound of a key in the door, footsteps on the stairs, her husband's voice. "Anybody home?"

"Only me," she said, standing up, not wanting to be caught napping. "Your wife." She stood up and gave him a long, protracted hug. "Sweet." he said, and laughed to himself. "Are you alright?"

"Yes, nostalgic, is all."

"Where's Junior, and my little girl? Not home yet?"

"Junior's at the chess club, and Miss beautiful just stepped out." she said, being careful with her words.

"Stepped out with who?"

"With that nice, shy boy who was here the other week, remember?"

"That tall, skinny boy who looks like he fell off a tobacco wagon, or something. I'll be damned—I was worried for a minute. I thought it might be something serious."

"Still waters run deep." her mother said softly.

"What?" He asked.

"Actually, I think your daughter's kind of smitten. You should have seen the way she ran out of here."

"Well, she better not be too smitten."

"She's almost seventeen, now. She has to have friends."

"Who said she shouldn't?"

"You—she was sort of seeing Herman for awhile, but you didn't like him."

"Because he wouldn't come up to visit. Besides, he's half a hoodlum. Hasn't made up his mind, yet, which way he's going."

"Well, Zak came up here and shook your hand."

"Yeah, but he forgot to look me in the eye. Plus, he's skinny, and, er, White."

"Oh, please, Calvin. It's 1994, in case you haven't checked a calendar, recently. Your views are a little passé, and we're not in North Carolina, anymore."

"Yeah, but we're still in *North* America, and that's good enough for me. Just ask Rodney King. And just because Slick Willie's in the White House, and plays a saxophone now and then and has a half Black baby somewhere, doesn't mean he's Black, either—sorry."

"It didn't seem to bother you too much, chasing light skinned women."

"Light, not white. There's a big difference," he said, but left it at that, not wanting to open up his past for review.

"Anyway, they're just friends, so relax. Just because you were running wild at seventeen doesn't mean everyone is . . . but she's at the age when she's going to start doing what she wants, anyway, regardless of what we say—just like I was, sneaking off to see you, against the objection of my entire family. They thought you were a bit on the dark side, if you remember."

"That was before they saw that I could take care of business, that I wasn't one of those trifling, yellow Negroes who were after you. They just didn't want black babies, that's all."

"It was five years before we stepped foot in my parents house, remember—I was two months pregnant with Ivy."

"All history—water over the dam. Now where's my paper?"

"Under your nose, if you care to look."

He picked it up from beside the chair beside him and sat heavily down, muttering. "Going for a walk!"

"More like a run, by the sound of it."

Not far from Ivy's house, over a hill and around a turn in the road and across a street or two, there was a small and sheltered park with a pond surrounded by a gravel path where people came to walk—old people, mostly, and mothers with strollers, a few joggers, and now and then a couple of teenagers like them. Zak and Ivy had walked slowly, not talking much, and it was only when they came into the small, sunlit space that she asked him what he had been doing in the neighborhood.

"You couldn't find a Twinkie nearer to your house?" Ivy asked.

"Yeah, but I couldn't find a beautiful girl to take a walk with."

"I'm sure you could of."

"I didn't want to."

"And where's my Twinkie?"

Zak looked guilty. "Oops," he said. "Sorry about that."

"False pretenses—that's alright. I don't like them anyway."

Ivy looked over at him, and they sat down on a bench in the sun. He was getting kind of bold these days, more confident.

"Your mother knew where you were going?" he asked her.

"Yeah, I told her."

"And?"

"Nothing. I think she kind of likes you, actually."

"And your dad?"

"Not home yet. He'll interrogate me when I get there, probably."

A cool wind swept across the park and lifted the corner of her skirt, held in place by a golden pin. The grass had not yet started to turn green, but few ambitious plants were pushing themselves up out of the moist, brown soil. The sun was warm, and when a swiftly moving cloud would pass across it, it would turn suddenly cold again, like March. Zak's arm lay across the top of the bench, behind her back, and he had to suppress the urge to let it fall across her shoulders like he wanted to. He looked over for a minute at her face—long eyelashes, the lovely, converging lines of her lips, the smooth skin of her neck descending to the wings of her collarbone.

"What?" she asked softly without looking up.

"What do you mean, what?"

"What are you looking at?"

"A beautiful girl."

"You think so?"

"I know so—you couldn't tell?"

"I thought you might of thought so, but were too shy to say. You stare a lot."

"Sorry—I can't help myself." Zak said, and then reached over and lightly took hold of her hand. "You're cold. We better go."

"You're not, I can see." she said, and didn't move her hand away. The sun reappeared with its warmth and he closed his eyes, then looked over at her as Ivy gazed away across the park, strands of her hair wavering around her face.

"Are you alright?" he asked.

"Yeah, I'm fine. Just tired, that's all."

They sat in silence for a minute and then Zak said, "There's something you should know about me. I have a confession, but I don't want to upset you."

"Try me." Ivy said.

"Are you sure you'll still like me?"

"I can't promise, but I'll try."

"It's been building for weeks—it's about my middle name."

Ivy studied his face, to see if he was being serious, "Break it to me gently, please."

"Promise?"

"Yes, I promise."

"It was my grandfather's, so don't laugh."

"Yeees . . . what *is* it, then? The suspense is killing me."

"Truman."

"Truman, like the president?" Ivy smiled. "That's alright—what's wrong with it?"

"I don't know—it always sounded funny, to me. Plus, they always called me 'Harry'. It drove me crazy. Now your turn."

"For what?"

"Middle name confession."

"Not so exciting: Dionna, with two n's . . ."

"That's nice."

"Yeah, I like it alright. Sometimes I wish that's what people called me. Truman: it's different. I like it—nice to meet you, Truman."

"You too, Dionna."

"We have no more secrets, then, do we?"

"Not that I can think of." They sat in silence, his warm hand lying on her cool one, and then with her other one she covered his with hers, tracing circles on his skin with her finger tips. He was trying to muster the courage to make a move, pull her closer to him still, when she took his hand, raised it slowly to her lips, and he watched as she softly kissed the back of his hand.

"There," she said, "I started it, so they can always blame me. Now, could you kiss me, please? The suspense is killing me."

Zak, though foolish, was no fool, and knew better than to answer with words. Instead, he pulled her towards him and leaned down toward her sunlit face, into the pocket of warmth that surrounded her, down toward the fragrance and smoothness of her skin. Her face was glowing, now, in the late afternoon sun, and the last thing Zak saw as his lips descended to meet hers was her eyes falling shut like two, translucent shells; and then his own eyes closed too, leaving his blind and trembling lips to find their way towards hers, as he gave himself over to a kind of bliss which, in all of his seventeen years until now, he had never known.

Perfume

In the days and weeks to follow, Zak's mother noticed there was something vaguely different about her son—a strange serenity, a lightness, or calm, she could not put her finger on. He spent more time out, somewhere else, but was more helpful around the house—washing dishes, taking out the trash—and sometimes when he came home from his mysterious whereabouts there was an unfamiliar fragrance about him that was neither tobacco, nor marijuana, but something closer to the scent of crushed flowers—perfume, of the kind worn by American teenaged girls towards the end of the second millennium, A.D.

She was cooking when he came in from somewhere, one day, the soft light of a spring afternoon fading in the window outside.

"Hi, mom." he said cheerfully. "What's for dinner?"

"Lamb chops—your favorite. How was school today?"

"Good." Zak said, and sensed she was fishing for more than this.

"And how are all your friends?"

"Which friends?"

"You know—Nick, for example."

"Oh, very good, Mom—Nick's the best, *you* know that—best beard in the whole school."

"No need to be sarcastic, Zachary."

"No—seriously. Nick rules."

"And Ivy?"

"*Ivy?* Also superb. I'll tell her you asked about her."

"Why don't you bring her over sometime?"

"For inspection, you mean?"

"No, but if she's one of your good friends, don't you think I should meet her? She sounds nice on the telephone."

"Thanks, Mom. I'll tell her you said so."

"Please do, and ask her what kind of perfume she wears—it's nice."

He was only half listening, but when she said this he perked up, blushed, and looked up; she was smiling, waiting for his reaction.

"Don't look so serious, Zachary. Mother's have a highly evolved sense of smell, you know."

"Apparently." Zak said. "I'll have to take up smoking again, as a precaution."

"No need for that."

"Alright, Mom. Why so many questions, anyway? You have problems with me and Ivy, too?"

"No, as a matter of fact, I don't, as long as you're happy, which you seem to be these days. In any case, you're very young—only in high school."

"Meaning what, we don't know any better?"

"No . . . but when people get older and start thinking about getting married, there are other things."

"Really? Like what, for example?"

"Oh, well, like money, where you're going to live, having children."

"Ah, er . . . not there yet, mom. I'm sixteen remember? I think I'm supposed to go to college first, and all that crap."

"Good idea."

"And we know about AIDS and condoms and getting pregnant—they've been beating us over the head with it since we were about four year's old, for Christ's sake."

"Don't swear, Zachary. And what about the race thing?"

"The 'race thing?' What would that be?"

"You know—she's Black and . . ."

"She's *Black*?!!" Zak said. "Oh my God! Now you tell me!" He watched his mother kind of half smile. Then he added, "Nobody cares about that anymore."

"Really?"

"Well, most people, anyway. Some of her so called friends gave her shit about it, called her a sellout, and all that crap. And some of the poor white trash over West Carver. I heard Heather got kicked out of her house for getting knocked up by some African dude. But other than that, no one."

"And how does Ivy deal with her friends?"

"She tries to ignore them. Yvonne gave her some shit one day, and they almost had a fight, and now they're not talking much." Zak paused. "Where'd you get all these strange ideas mom, anyway?"

"I'm American—we're born with it. It used to be a bigger deal, especially for the White family. They would disown their own children, deny their grandchildren. Back in the sixties they used to say that children from mixed marriages had a hard time at school—other kids would call them names, stuff like that. And the kids themselves could be confused."

"About what?"

"Their racial identity, I suppose."

"Gee, mom, sounds like a bunch of bull to me . . . maybe back in the day, when you were growing up, wearing your beads and flower dresses and smoking weed. Most kids my age don't care about all that anymore. They're too busy buying new sneakers and trying to look cool. Everyone's mixed, anyway. That's what they tell us in biology class, anyway. Races don't exist. Someone made it all up."

She smiled. "That's good news: now all we have to do is convince eight billion other people, or so. Maybe the world *is* improving, slightly—you wouldn't think so from watching the news. In any case, she sounds very nice, and you seem very happy these days, so I'm happy for that—that's all I really wanted to say. And I'd love to meet her sometime, if you want to bring her over for dinner, since she seems to make you happy."

"Well, maybe I'm happy because I got a B—on my last trigonometry test, up from a C. And sure, I can invite Ivy over, and her parents, too, and we can have a big symposium on teenaged relationships in the nineties.

"No need to get excited." She said, amused by his little tirade. "Have you met her family?"

"Yeah, I've been to their house. Her mother's cool. I met her father, briefly. I liked him, too, but I don't think he'd be too happy with the thought of his beautiful, only daughter hanging out with the likes of me."

"Or *any* boy, for that matter. It's not easy being a father, you know."

"So I've noticed. Just look at mine."

"Well, that's a whole other story. But if I were you, I'd try to not be smelling of his daughter's perfume the next time you meet him."

"Thanks for the tip, Mom. That's probably a good idea." He watched her round up the lamb chops, green beans, rice, slide them onto plates, and sit down at the table. She looked pretty, but tired.

"How *close* are you two, anyway?"

Zak looked up. "Don't worry, Mom—we walk around a lot and sit on park benches. We don't have a car, so it's not like Vermont, where you drive around in your daddy's pickup truck looking for the nearest hay stack to lie in. Besides, we're nerds."

"No you're not, and neither is she. She's actually very beautiful."

"You think so?"

"Of course—it's obvious." She looked down at her books. "In any case, there are other things to worry about—like this test I'm taking tomorrow."

"You'd better study, Mom—can't have you flunking out, and bringing shame upon the entire family. Think of *my* reputation. No one will even talk to me."

"Alright," she said, sitting down, "Now eat."

"Yes, mother, I shall."

Sanctuary

One hundred and something years before, or so, a Professor of botany at Carver University convinced the board of trustees of the need to purchase a large tract of land for an arboretum, for the study, protection, and cultivation of trees from all over the world. The land, in what was then the rural fringes of the city, was bought from an elderly farmer and designed by the great landscape architect, Frederick Law Olmstead who, true to his promise, populated the few hundred acres of woods and fields and hills with trees from all over the planet, a couple of small ponds, a road and various paths winding among them. This, and more, Zak and Ivy learned one Saturday afternoon in April when, without knowing where they were going, took the subway to the end of the line, out beyond into the fringes of the city. At the final stop they saw a small sign that pointed up a hill to the park, where they walked around for an hour or more—slowly, along the paths, through the groves of trees and small meadows, up and over a hill and then down again to where a stream passed through a small valley full of pine trees that reminded Zak of what it might look like out in Colorado, or Utah, or the French Alps, one of those places he always wanted to go skiing, one day.

After that initial discovery, that beautiful April afternoon, they would go there once or twice a week, on weekends or sunny afternoons after school, and walk around for a couple hours, and stop at the familiar places—on a bench, or at the top of the hill they called "the mountain" to watch the sun set, or the joggers huff and puff up the hill and, without stopping, turn around and run down. It was a place where nobody knew them, and where they knew nobody, and where, when they passed people on the paths, they would just say hello, or smile, and in this small way, seemed to give them their blessing, made them feel anonymous and welcome—a place where they could just be themselves, far from the crush and complications of school and home and all the places in between.

"The sanctuary," Ivy called it, and called the places they liked to stop their sacred places, and gave them all their names: 'the stream', 'the forest', 'the pines', 'the meadows', 'the rock." Zak liked best a forest of small, unusual looking pine trees, that reminded him of Colorado, or Austria, like some kind of alpine meadow, and he half expected Heidi to appear, singing as she walked amidst the trees. There, they would find a secluded place in a shifting patch of sunlight, and sometimes they brought a blanket and would sit and talk, or not talk, or lie on their backs and watch the sky, the shifting clouds, like the whole world was tilting on its axis. As they lay, Ivy would all of a sudden go silent, and when Zak looked over at her, he would realize she had fallen asleep, her chest rising and falling, and he would watch her, or lay his arm across her and fall into a kind of half sleep himself. The sun made her drowsy. "Yes, Zachary . . ." She would say suddenly, surprising him, and then deny that she had ever been asleep, that she only 'resting,' as she liked to put it. "Just don't let a squirrel walk on me, that's all I ask. I'm not at one with nature like you are." He would pull her towards him then, aware of the shape her body made in his arms, the way their bodies seem to fit together, fold into each other, like they were meant to be that way. And then their lips would meet, and they would kiss without words—only the wind in the pine trees above them, or an unnamed animal, scurrying in leaves nearby, or the voices of people at a distance, talking, footsteps walking nearby, not stopping to look at them—two young lovers lying on the warming earth. He was amazed, at first, at the varied and surprising things that could happen when two peoples lips met, and he would sometimes have to stop and catch his breath and just look at her—her skin, her lips, the light wisps of down on her cheeks, her hair so soft to the touch, like silk, a texture he had never known before. He never tired of kissing her, of holding her, or of the way her hand sought out his as they lay, the way her body felt against his. And then, without their noticing, the shadows would lengthen, the air would turn slightly cooler, and without a word they would stand up, brush the pine needles and flecks of pine cones and other artifacts of nature of their clothes and hair, and start the slow walk through the fading light, back to the subway, and home.

On the train people would look at them, to see if they were really 'together' or not, and at such moments he would put his arm around her, or hold her hand, to help them with their answer. When they got to his stop he wouldn't get off, but would take it two more, to hers, kiss her goodbye at the turn style, watch her until she was gone, and then take the train back in the other direction, and walk slowly home, smelling of pine needles and grass and the fragrant earth where they had lain.

Stay Beautiful

That spring there were three new babies born to the youthful students at Carver High School and among the new mothers was Heather, and to no one's surprise the child, a girl, was a beautiful shade of brown. "Amber" would be her name.

Her parents, it was said, were furious, less about the baby than its complexion, but after a couple of weeks a distant relative remarked that the girl looked rather like Heather's father, and the family consensus softened. It came as an astonishing revelation that a brown baby could look like its White grandfather, but there it was—the same mouth, the same furrowed brow, the same dimple on her cheeks.

The father of the child, once rumored to be a Haitian taxi driver, in fact turned out to be a Senegalese graduate student of European History, and now and then they could be seen, all three of them, strolling in the soft, spring sunshine across the campus. Heather's parents asked only that the three of them not stroll the streets of her own neighborhood, where the sight of their café au lait daughter and Black lover might not be such a great idea.

In the park outside the school, the bare branches of the trees were touched with green, and the dead and trampled grass had begun to show signs of life. After school teenagers gathered in their little knots and clusters, and small birds hopped around on the ground, looking for worms to tug out of the sun-warmed soil.

Ivy and Zak had given up sneaking out the back and meeting at the college, and met instead on a bench at the far side of the park. They were sitting one afternoon, in the sunlight, when Heather came by with a squeaky stroller that held a sleeping baby with long eyelashes and tight curly hair.

"Is this the inter-racial dating bench?" she asked, reminding Zak that there was something about her he had always found annoying.

"No, actually, it's just a normal, wooden bench," he said. "Anyone can sit here, even unwed mothers." Ivy glanced over at him and raised her eyebrow: it was usually she who had a sharp tongue.

"No thanks." Heather said. "We have to go see my baby daddy." She uttered this peculiar phrase with a certain pride, as if he had no other connection to her.

"What's his name," Zak asked, "your baby daddy?" Ivy nudged him lightly in the ribs.

"Jean-Claude." Heather said, and then added, in explanation, "Senegal used to be French. I prefer his tribal name—Osman." She looked different since she had the baby—fuller, older, tired. "See you guys later. I've got to go."

"If you ever need a baby sitter," Ivy offered, "let me know. Zak would be happy to, I'm sure."

"Eight dollars an hour," Zak said.

"A day, maybe." Heather said. "I'm broke." As she walked away, the stroller made a pleasant crunching sound on the sand left from winter. From a distance, Heather looked like just a woman wearily pushing a stroller—nothing teenaged about her.

"Don't give her a hard time." Ivy chastised Zak. "It's not easy, you know."

"I didn't ask her to have a baby. There are ways to avoid it."

"Oh, really—you're an expert?"

"No, but . . . she started it, with that interracial bench crap joke."

"It was a just a joke." Ivy said.

"A lame one." Zak said, and was about to put his arm around her, right there, for all to see, when they heard a car honking once behind them, and then again. Ivy looked over her shoulder.

"Jesus, I think it's my father. What's he doing here?"

"Oops", Zak said, and Ivy got up quickly, and walked back to the large white car, idling by the curb. "Hi, Dad," she said, looking in through the open window. "What are you doing here?"

"Nothing, beautiful. Just driving by. I thought I'd see if you were around— nice day, and all."

After a moment's uncertainty Zak had gotten up, and followed her slowly to the car.

"You remember Zak, Dad, don't you?" she asked. "You met at the house, once."

"Sure I do," he said, looking out at Zak. "How are you, young man?"

"Oh, I'm fine. Thank you, Mr. Whitman." Zak said, "Nice to see you."

"Likewise," he said, and then to Ivy. "Hop in—I'll take you home."

"Actually, Dad, we have to go back in to school for a study group meeting."

"What time?"

"Three thirty, or so."

"Good, it's only three ten—I'll have you back here in a few minutes. You don't mind, do you, Mr. ah . . . Zachary, do you?"

"Sure—of course not. I have to go back in now, anyway."

"I'll be back in a little while." Ivy said, looked at Zak and rolled her eyes, and climbed in with a strange sense of foreboding. They drove off with the familiar, airy whoosh, and beside her father Ivy felt very slight and small, suddenly, like a balloon that had just lost its air; she wondered what was going on, what the point of all this was, and it did not help that her father did not say anything, just drove in silence, steering this wide American car through the leafy streets of the city beneath a canopy of newly leafing trees.

He drove slowly away from the school, then past the college, and through the square, down toward the river—the same route that Zak and Ivy took on their long, meandering walks after school. He had not picked her up like this since she was in third grade, and he had the radio on low, to those love songs his parents had listened to when they were young, from the seventies, long before she was born.

A sudden rush of fear came into her—she thought of her mother—her grandmother. "Everything's alright, isn't it?" Ivy asked. "Nothing bad happened to anyone, did it?"

"Oh, no, nothing like that." He said, and glanced over at her, "Just driving around—thinking. It's been a while since we talked—life's so busy these days." It seemed he was going to say something else, but then he lapsed back into thought. The car swung onto the drive, and then they swept along beside the river where a few boats from the college team were out, their oars dipping down into the water in unison, like a giant dragon fly. A few joggers were lumbering along over the soft warm earth. Ivy looked over at him again. She was getting nervous. "Did you have something you wanted to say to me, Daddy? The suspense is killing me. This is kind of odd."

"Odd?" he said, though not in an unpleasant way. "A father and his only daughter taking a drive on a beautiful day in the spring of her sixteenth—I mean seventeenth—year? Not too odd, I wouldn't think, taking a few minutes out of their busy lives."

"I know, but . . ." Ivy couldn't finish her thought.

Again, he did not answer immediately, but mulled the question over to himself. When she looked over, a strange softness had taken over his face, an expression she had last seen at the funeral of his great aunt, back in North Carolina, as they both looked down onto her body as it lay in the coffin, surrounded by flowers.

"Do I?" he asked softly, "Good question. I guess I do want to say something, though I'm not sure what it is, exactly, not sure I can find the right words, at the moment." He paused for a minute, and then continued. "I guess I want to say that you're my only daughter, and I—your mother and I both—want the best for you, don't want you or your brother to suffer the hardships that we had to, growing up. We don't want you to get hurt by anyone, or anything." He paused again, and Ivy felt something rising up in her, too, she had to fight it back.

"Your friend there, old Zachary . . ." he continued, "He seems like a nice enough fellow, and I have nothing against him personally. And I know it's supposed to be different, for you kids, different generation and all that, but the jury's still out, on that one—I'll believe it when I see it with my own eyes. But when we were growing up, your mother and I, White men only wanted one thing from our women, and once he got it, it was back to business as usual— back to being his maid, or cook, or whatever else you were, and that was it. And for a Black man, if you looked at a White woman wrong, or got a little fresh, you could end up at the bottom of a river before you knew what hit you—just like Emmett Till. I'm not saying it's like that now, up here, anyway, but this country moves about as fast as a glacier, sometimes, when it comes to some things, and that's one of them, as far as I'm concerned."

Ivy was going to answer, to say something, like, "What does that have to do with me—that's the past, over, history, goodbye? Time to get over it." But as she watched his face, struggling to find the words, she could feel that something start to well up in her, again, some strange, sweet sorrow, but she tried to fight it off, keep it down, away. Outside, the river flowed by in slow motion, and Ivy knew that what she saw now, what she was looking at, would be frozen in memory for the rest of her life: a bunch of kids, looking at stuff, by the river's edge, a few people walking dogs, an old man on a bicycle pedaling slowly upstream, the white petals of a tree in bloom blowing off in the wind, falling to the ground like flakes of snow.

Her father continued, his voice lighter now. "There was this girl back in my hometown, come to think of it, when I was about fourteen, fifteen years old, maybe. We were in the same class in school. Nice, pretty, blond hair, green eyes, good figure—the whole thing. Mary her name was. I used to see her on my way home from school, and we used to be friendly, talk a little. She would smile at me, and say hi. I was kind of sweet on her, and I'm pretty sure it was mutual, and I was trying to get up my nerve, fool that I was, trying to figure out how I could spend some time with her, and one day these boys with slicked back hair and white socks and pointed black shoes and pants a little too short, like there was a flood or something, started following me home after school, asking me how Mary was doing, and didn't I know that one of them was her brother? No I didn't, I told them, and I didn't know how she was doing, since I didn't talk to her. They kind of shrugged that off, and got a little closer to me, and asked, didn't I have a younger sister, Agnes, and asked me how she was doing, and then one of them said she was sort of pretty, 'for a black girl', and wasn't I scared something bad could happen to her, one day? I played ignorant, of course, and just kept walking, and they fell back, and stood there, kind of laughing as I walked away. Well, that kind of cured me of my desire to get closer to Mary. Eventually, she married one of those nice fellows, one of her brother's best friends, but he used to beat her up every night when he got home from work, as her reward for marrying a good White man. Eventually she got tired of that and left him, and I heard years later that she married a Black man and moved to Chicago. She had three children by him, but her family disowned her, and denied the children. Too late—she was gone."

He steered his car to the left, crossed over a bridge that spanned the river, and then turned back on the other side. "So that's where *I'm* coming from. When I was coming up, you tried to be friends with a White girl, and they offer to shoot you instead, do something to your younger sister. Thirty years later, you're supposed to hand over your only daughter with a smile, and say, "Yes, that's all in the past, all forgotten, all forgiven. This is the land of the *good* White people, now, and here's my beautiful sixteen year old daughter, getting all A's at the high school and going to be a doctor, or lawyer someday, and I know you don't mean any harm, and by the way, here are the keys to my car, and take her for a nice drive in the country, if you want to, and . . ."

"Stop, Daddy, please," Ivy pleaded, and that's when the thing that was welling up in her burst loose, finally, and she could feel the tears suddenly flooding down her cheeks, filling the palms of her cupped hands as she pressed them to her face, and then she was weeping like a child, taking air in breathless gasps, and she could feel his strong arm around her shoulders, pulling her to him. "Now, now," he said. "Don't you start up, too."

"None of this was planned, daddy," she said between sobs. "It just happened. I can't help how I feel. We just get along, that's all—we're friends."

"Enough, baby. I know all that—this isn't about you, so much as me. I'm just trying to explain myself now, so you can understand. I'm not so perfect myself, as your mother likes to remind us—especially when I was younger. I know what boys can be like, but your friend seems like a nice enough fellow. I like the way he came over and said hello—that says something to me, right there. But go slowly, that's all I'm trying to say. Don't love anyone more than you love yourself. It's a tough world out there, and we don't want you getting hurt. Your mother's working on me, and she says he's a nice young man, and so I'm trying. Now reach into that glove compartment and get some tissue, and pull yourself together—I don't want anyone thinking I whooped you or anything." Ivy laughed, and wiped her tears and looked at herself in the mirror: she looked older, like she had just aged ten years in ten minutes, her eyes wet and rimmed with red.

The large car swung away from the river, and headed up through the leafy neighborhood toward the school. "And if you're going to be friends with old Zachary—and I guess you are already—you tell him we want to see him around the house sometimes, so we can fatten him up a little. He's kind of skinny. That's all."

Ivy laughed through her tears, and felt she should say something else, to answer him, but how? As they drove the final couple blocks to the school, he slowed down even more, as if he didn't want their drive to be over, but then he finally eased up to the curb, in the exact spot where he had picked her up twenty minutes before. It seemed as though a year had passed. The bench was empty.

"Now go study." he said. "Keep up your grades. We're all proud of you."

Ivy reached over and held his arm, and could feel the tears coming back. "None of this was planned." she repeated softly.

"Shhh . . . enough. You don't have to explain." Her father said. "Life is never planned."

"I'll be home for dinner." she said, but then, struck by the banality of her comment, blurted out "I love you, Daddy,"—words she had not spoken since she was a child. And she wept again, suddenly and uncontrollably, and leaned against him, and his strong arm surrounded her and pulled her to him. "I love you too, baby. Now give me a hug, and go on, unless you want to see a grown man cry. I could be court-martialed." Ivy laughed again, and wiped her eyes, glanced in the mirror, and opened the door, and then slid out of the car. She looked back in at him. "You'll be fine," he said, and he winked, "I'm proud of you. Stay beautiful."

And then she watched as the car pulled away, like an ocean liner leaving port in an old, black and white movie, and suddenly she wanted him not to leave, wanted to be back in the car beside him, still with him, wanted to be driving through the pleasant, tree lined streets of her childhood, when the world seemed simpler, safer, but it was too late. She stood by the curb and watched as the car moved away, swept around the corner, and was gone.

May

Then it was May—the month of Ivy's birth. On the twenty sixth, she would be seventeen.

Inside the school one morning Zak found the usual cacophony of sounds—voices, shrieks, laughter, singing, slamming lockers, running feet, the voice of Mrs. Williams, a short affable hall monitor, built like a fire hydrant, exhorting everyone to get to their homerooms. "Ladies and gentlemen! You have exactly two and one half minutes to get to your classrooms!!" Zak got his books and walked slowly through the halls. He turned into room 203 and sat down at the same cluster of desks where, for the last seven months, he had been sitting, at a desk etched with the graffiti and hieroglyphs of those who had come before him, had passed through the halls of the school, then disappeared, like prehistoric beasts falling off the edge of some cliff, never to be seen again. What happened to kids when they graduated, or didn't graduate, as the case may be? Where did they go afterwards? He opened his book to study, but every time someone came in, he looked up with a quiet sense of anticipation, but when he looked up next it was not Ivy but Yvonne that he saw, her hair done up in the swoopy style of the fashion magazines, busting out of a tight black sweater. She glanced at him, and he thought he heard her suck her teeth. Ivy and Yvonne didn't really talk anymore, though Yvonne had made few half hearted attempts to revive their injured friendship.

Then Mr. Turnbull came racing in with his usual white shirt and stiff necktie and hair kept neatly in place with some hair stuff everyone joked about—"Mr. Frozen-locks," they called him. He looked like someone straight out of the nineteen fifties, one of those corny characters who showed up in black and white every now and then on cable television late at night. Zak looked up to watch the last seconds tick off, the minute hand jump to 8:22, and then the music started, and Mr. Turnbull went through the familiar litany of names for about the one hundred and fiftieth time that year, like an old, tired poem: "Vipond, David—yup; Valmond, Rosita—good morning, Ms. Valmond; Walker, Zak—yes; Whitman, Ivy," he said, looked up and was about the mark her absent when Ivy came quickly into the room and said, "here," and Mr. Turnbull said, "tardy—as usual." and Ivy, looking flushed and harried, sat down heavily in the seat across from Zak, and said "Whatever."

"Greetings." Zak said quietly.

"Good morning," she said, catching her breath.

Mr. Turnbull continued: "And those of you who are planning to go to the Junior Prom, you must have your money in by the end of next week, or you can't go—no exemptions."

"*Exceptions*," Ivy corrected him, but he didn't hear her.

"What prom?" Zak asked.

"The Junior Prom, I believe. You haven't heard?"

"I wasn't invited, yet."

Ivy looked at him sadly. "You're a Junior—you're invited. Now *you're* supposed to invite someone. That's the custom, I believe, even now, in 1994."

He watched her now as she settled in—stood up, pulled off her coat, sat down, wiped the sweat from her forehead. A week before, she suddenly cut off all her hair at a men's barber shop, and wore it now in a short natural, about half an inch long; Zak had been surprised, and so had her parents and friends but, after the initial shock and a few strange comments, they had gotten used to it, and Zak had realized she looked even more beautiful than before.

"*I* like it." Ivy had said at the time. "If other people don't, that's their problem—they have their hair, I have mine. And I'm tired of combing it out, getting perms."

Beside, you could see her face better now, and the shape of her head, and graceful arc of her neck as it descended to her shoulders, and he loved to run his hands over the smooth softness of her hair. But it was her eyes, Zak had long since decided, that made her so beautiful—their perfect almond shape, a slight, inward tilt, like French accents, and their color, a lighter brown touched with flecks of yellow, orange, gold. Her cheeks had flushed slightly, from her last minute dash to school, and from lying with Zak for an hour or two the afternoon before. A couple of freckles had appeared on her high cheekbones. She wore no makeup, no lipstick, even, on the lips that Zak had come to know better than his own.

In these few, brief minutes of homeroom he liked to remember how it had been before he knew her, before they had ever spoken—back when he sat and watched her trying to think of things to say to her, trying not to sound like a dope. "Excuse me, could I borrow your pencil, please?" Or, "Do you know what our homework was?" Or, "It's nice out today, isn't it?" Even now they didn't talk much during homeroom, in part because they still maintained a pretense of secrecy, distance, as if what they shared was too fragile to be revealed.

"May I help you, young man?" Ivy said now, looking up at him. "You seem to be staring."

"Sorry—I'm just resting my eyes. You're pretty."

"What did you say your name was, again? You're very bold."

"I have no name. I'm from Vermont. People call me Olney—that's where I'm from."

"That's nice. I'm Ivy, like the vine."

"Like the vine." Zak said. He was leaning forward on his desk, watching her face while Mr. Turnbull nattered on about the end of the semester—"Not to mention the millennium—only six years to go. The end of the world is at hand, Armageddon, and we're all going to roast in the eternal fires of hell—some of us. But you should try to graduate, anyway—life will be easier for you that way." He waited for a laugh, but no one was really listening.

"And how did you sleep?" Zak asked.

"Alright, but I dreamt I was lying in the grass with some tall, shy boy who kept kissing me, like he was going to eat me up . . ."

"How terrible"

"Not really." Ivy said. "It wasn't so bad. He had nice gray eyes."

"Not blue?" he asked.

"A little blue—mostly gray."

She was wearing a sweater dress made of a kind of slightly shiny wool that made you want to touch it, and when she stood up for a second to look for something in her bag, the contours of her body rose up before him—the smooth skin of her legs rising to the swelling of her hips, and then up to her narrow waist, the subtle concavity where her belly button was. "Hmmmm . . ." Zak said.

"Are you singing?"

"Just humming to myself." When she sat down, he reached across beneath the table and scissor-ed her legs between his and pulled her towards him.

"Help, help . . ." she said.

"It's a nice dress you're wearing."

"You think so?" Ivy said, glancing down at herself. "My mother doesn't."

"Not surprising," Zak said. "Would you like to go to the prom?"

"But we just met—are *you* inviting me?"

"I'm trying to."

"Well, try again."

"Ah, excuse me, miss, would you like to be my escort to the prom, please?"

"No, but you can be *my escort*—I think that's the way it works. I'll have to get a dress."

"You have a closet full of them."

"Been snooping, have you? I see you know nothing about women." Ivy said.

"I only know what I'm told, or shown," he said, but she left that one alone.

In a month it would be summer, and then what? He had planned to go back to Olney to paint houses with his best friend, Parker, but he was already plotting ways to stay in the city, get a job, summer school—whatever. Ivy was going south for a few weeks to see her family in North Carolina, and then would return and look for a job, to start to save for college.

He watched her, now, as she turned a silver bracelet around and around on her slender wrist—a bracelet, only they knew, that he had given her a month before. As she did so he noticed that underneath the silver her skin, hidden from the sun, had remained a shade or two of lighter brown.

"You're getting darker."

"Oh yes—Black people do you know. It's a little known fact. You don't like it?"

"Yes, I do, actually."

"You're too kind." She had always loved being out in the sun, loved the way it felt on her skin, and this summer, she had decided, she would stop hiding from the sun, and let herself become the color that she really was, a deeper, richer shade of brown.

When the music started everyone stood up, but Zak just sat there and watched as Ivy gathered her books, draped her coat over her arm, headed for the door, then turned.

"See you later?"

"I hope so," Zak said, "Same place?"

"If you wish."

"I wish." Zak said, and then watched her as she walked out of the room—a pretty girl in a knit wool dress pressed outward into the shape of a woman. At the door she turned and waved, as she often did, and then was carried away by the students who ebbed and flowed through the school like the tides.

June

If you happened to be sitting on a bench outside Carver Public High School, one particular evening at the beginning of June, 1994, you might have been surprised by the sight of well dressed teenagers, boys in tuxedos and girls in long, beautiful dresses, some black, others purple, or magenta, or mauve, or turquoise, shimmering as they walked across the criss-crossing pathways of the park towards the school. There was something unexpected in the sight, and if you just happened to be feeding the pigeons or something, and squinted, you might think that these well well-dressed people, talking and laughing as they strolled through the sunlight and shadow cast by the pale green leaves of spring, weren't teenagers at all but the grownups they would soon be. Among them was Nick, the bearded wonder, looking not so much like an addled pothead as an English gentleman of the eighteenth century: he had trimmed his hair, and beard, and was wearing a nice old-styled tuxedo, and an old top hat. Furthermore, he appeared to be walking with a woman in a long, beige dress with small, embroidered flowers. She had long, blond hair, and wore no make up, and looked like the women in one of Shakespeare's plays, *A Mid Summer Night's Dream.*

"Look, there's Nick," Zak said to Ivy from the back seat of the limousine in which they were both sitting. "And he seems to actually have a date."

"Why shouldn't he—he's a nice guy," Ivy said. "Look how good he looks, when he wants to."

"Which is about once a year."

"Actually," Ivy said suggestively, "I think he's kind of cute, these days."

"Last stop." Herman said, for that was who they were riding with in the limo—Herman and Sonia, and a friend of his, from the basketball team, Jimmy Petite, and his date, Marie, who was wearing the shiniest, reddest dress Zak had ever seen. Sonia looked voluptuous, too, in a dark blue, satiny dress with lacy fringes and a low neckline, revealing to all her beautiful bust, "poitrine", as Zak had learned in French class. "In France, this is very important." Mme Maillard had said, looking down at her own.

136

Yeah, in France and everywhere else in the world, too. Zak had thought, but did not say.

"Midnight?" asked the driver, who worked for Herman's uncle, who owned the car and the company. Two days earlier Herman had asked Ivy if she wanted to come with them, and so they had. And now, all six of them spilled out, and joined the others walking across the park to the gym. Ivy too, was beautiful, in her short hair and her pendulous gold earrings, in a dress of a pale, ethereal blue, like the color of the sky on spring mornings, with subtle, white, floral patterns sewn into the cloth. As they walked she had looped her arm through his, and pulled him close to her. She looked older, as Zack imagined she would ten years into the future.

There had been an effort, that spring, to move the prom from its traditional location at school to some fancy restaurant, like "Jimmy's Pier Four," where the senior prom was held, but in the end they had decided to hold it here, in the old tired gym. The committee had done its best to spruce the place up, and if you squinted, you would hardly recognize it through the streamers, and balloons, and the soft lights and the round tables with white table clothes and flowers in the middle—a magical kingdom of possibility. There was a DJ set up, already, and a stage where a band would appear, to which the prom king and queen would be summoned.

Zak was impressed by the transformation of his classmates—the motley assemblage of bedraggled youth transformed into a fashion show of handsome young men and beautiful women, with lots of bare backs and belly button rings and new tattoos that disappeared down the backs of their dresses, down into that lovely concavity at the base of the spine, where the lower back, he had recently discovered, rises up into the soft, deep curves of other places, whose mysteries were slowly being revealed.

Some teachers were there too, equally transformed: Ms. Newman, in an African print dress, her baby dreadlocks getting longer, and Mme Maillard, looking even more ravishing than usual, wearing a long dress the color of Ivy's skin, and little else, it seemed to the naked eye, underneath.

"I swear, from the back, she could be Black," someone said.

"Hey, that's a stereotype." Zak said with mock indignation.

"True," Ivy said, "And I don't like stereotypes, but some of them are true, and, let's face it, the big booty theory is one of them. Scientists have studied it."

"Really?" Zak said, "Fascinating. Maybe I'll try harder in biology next year."

Nick appeared, still looking like he had walked out of some book, or TV show on public television.

"Nick-meister—what's up? Where'd you get your threads? You look like Charles Dickens, or something."

"They were my uncle's—before he was dead. Then he gave them to me. I'm the only one they fit."

"And the lid?"

"My grandfather's, and his father's before that. A family heirloom."

"And who's the hot chick you're with?"

"Oh, that's Marianna. She doesn't go here."

"And are you two, ah, er, *an item*?" Zak asked.

"Ask me in about five hours," Nick said, looking at his watch. "I should know by then."

"Geesh! I guess even a blind squirrel finds a nut, sometimes." Zak said, and Ivy kicked him under the table. Nick just smiled. "Blind, but happy."

"I'm just playing. You look great together, I must admit."

"You, too, dude. Which reminds me—I better get back before she bounces without me. Later."

Along one wall there was a bar set up where you could buy fancy, non-alcoholic drinks with exotic sounding names that made you feel like you were drunk, even if you weren't. "Do you want something? I'm kind of thirsty." Zak asked, getting up.

"Oh, yes. A Virgin Mary, perhaps." Ivy said.

"Sounds good." He wondered if this was an oblique confession, of some sort. They had never really discussed the subject, though he had wondered, and she had wondered where he had learned to kiss in a way that made her feel as though she was melting, or floating, as though she wanted all of her clothes to suddenly evaporate, or melt off of her, or fall to her feet, leaving her unclothed body to follow its own aspirations.

"What are you thinking about?" he asked when he returned.

She was smiling to herself. "A secret. I'll show you—I mean *tell* you— later."

"I can't wait." Food appeared on the tables, then disappeared into the bodies of ravenous teenagers, and then the music began, and everyone drifted towards the dance floor, watching a bunch of boys from the downwardly mobile crowd, not so much dancing as mugging, posturing, posing, in some peculiar ritual, jostling each other around the floor in a strange knot of adolescent male energy. But then they stopped the music, and the class President, Ruben Badillo, stood up, and said it was time for everyone to start dancing, and later they would announce the prom king and queen.

Then the lights were dimmed, better music came on, three girls walked out onto the dance floor, and, sensing their moment, boys followed like magnets, and everyone nearby moved out onto the floor, in the swirling, moving mass of tuxedo-ed, sequined teenaged bodies. "Ready?" she asked him.

"For?" Zak said.

Ivy rolled her eyes. "You're not going to pull this Mr. Shy thing on me, are you? I didn't come here to watch." She grabbed his hand and pulled him up and through the crowd into the middle of the room.

Suspended above the dance floor was a shiny, revolving globe composed of thousands of tiny mirrors, and as they danced wands of light passed through the crowd, illuminating parts of people—a hand, a breast, a glittering brooch, a bare, tattooed back with a hand on it. He could see, also, glimpses of people he had gotten to know that year, like a moving picture album—there was Nick and 'his lady' dancing is such a way that seemed to indicate romantic entanglement; Herman, already in a swaying bear hug with Sonia, going for prom queen; and even Heather was there with her boyfriend, having gotten her mother to baby sit for him. Yvonne was working the crowd, moving through the room like a great gust of wind, or fire, letting different men dance with her for about two and half minutes each before she would push them off and move on to someone else, their gathering ardor getting too high to contain. Then a slow song came on, and those with no one to latch on to quietly dispersed, while the lovers among them, or the would-be's and the wanna-be's or gonna-be's, moved out onto the floor, and Zak slid into Ivy's arms. They fell into an easy rhythm, Zak remembering the one dancing lesson Ivy had given him— one long slow move to the left, then a kind of pause, wait, then back the other way, in a slow sensuous roll of her hips.

"Slowwly . . ." she had admonished him, "What's your hurry?" He now followed the cadence of her body as she moved, the pause of her hips at the top of every beat, the sweet friction of her body against his. He was aware of her hands on the small of his back, and the warmth of her skin, the soft, ambiguous pressure of her breasts against him. His hand had settled on the small of her bare, warm back, and the other on her shoulder, the nape of her neck as it ascended to the wonderful soft down of her hair, and as they danced Zak was aware of feeling acutely, almost painfully happy, as he generally did when he was with her, in the soft, private kingdom of her room, under the watchful eyes of the Teddy bears, in those rare moments when the house was empty, and they lay on the bed together, then the sound of the key in the door, footsteps, and they would move, swiftly, back to the living room where they were supposed to be.

He looked to his right, over her shoulder, and there, across the room, saw a couple he did not recognize—a tall, pale boy, holding on for dear life to a slender, pretty girl with very short hair and a slight, subtle body, swathed in a shiny blue dress: "You're smiling." Ivy said. "What is it?"

"I just saw this weird looking couple, over there."

"Where?" Ivy said.

"There—a pretty girl dancing with some geek in a Tuxedo."

"They look fine to me." Ivy said.

"She does—it's him I'm worried about."

Ivy looked over at the mirror. "He looks OK, too," she said. ". . . for a country boy."

"You're too kind." Zak said.

And now her fingers were tracing slow, languorous circles on his back, and for a moment he closed his eyes and let himself stop thinking, let his body follow the slow, sensuous motion of hers, her thighs, swathed in satin, or silk, slowly scissoring against his. "Ouch." he said.

"What's the matter?"

"Sweet, sweet." he said softly, something she had whispered to him, sometimes, after they kissed and lay together in one of their sacred places, catching their breath, the warmth and weight of her pulled against him. And now he did not want the song to end, this moment amidst this pleasant, motley hodgepodge of teenage humanity; but then it was over, finally, the song whimpering off into a sad, sweet decrescendo of love and teenage heartbreak, and he awoke from his trance and the couples around them began to release each other and file back to their tables. But he held on to her for a moment longer, and then they, too, walked off the dance floor, but his strange, weightless sensation remained—a happiness so sweet it pained him to think it would not last forever. "You know," he said, feeling the need to say something, to fill the silence, to bring himself back down to earth. "This is kind of corny."

"I know," Ivy said, her hand finding its way to his, "But that's alright—it's supposed to be. Life just is, sometimes."